TALES OF THE LOST HORIZON

AN *Illustrated Collection* OF
Speculative Short Stories AND *Poetry*

MICHAEL EGING

Book Design by HMDpublishing

ISBN: 978-0-9887099-3-5

Cover Design: http://www.selfpubbookcovers.com/vikncharlie

FEATURED ARTISTS

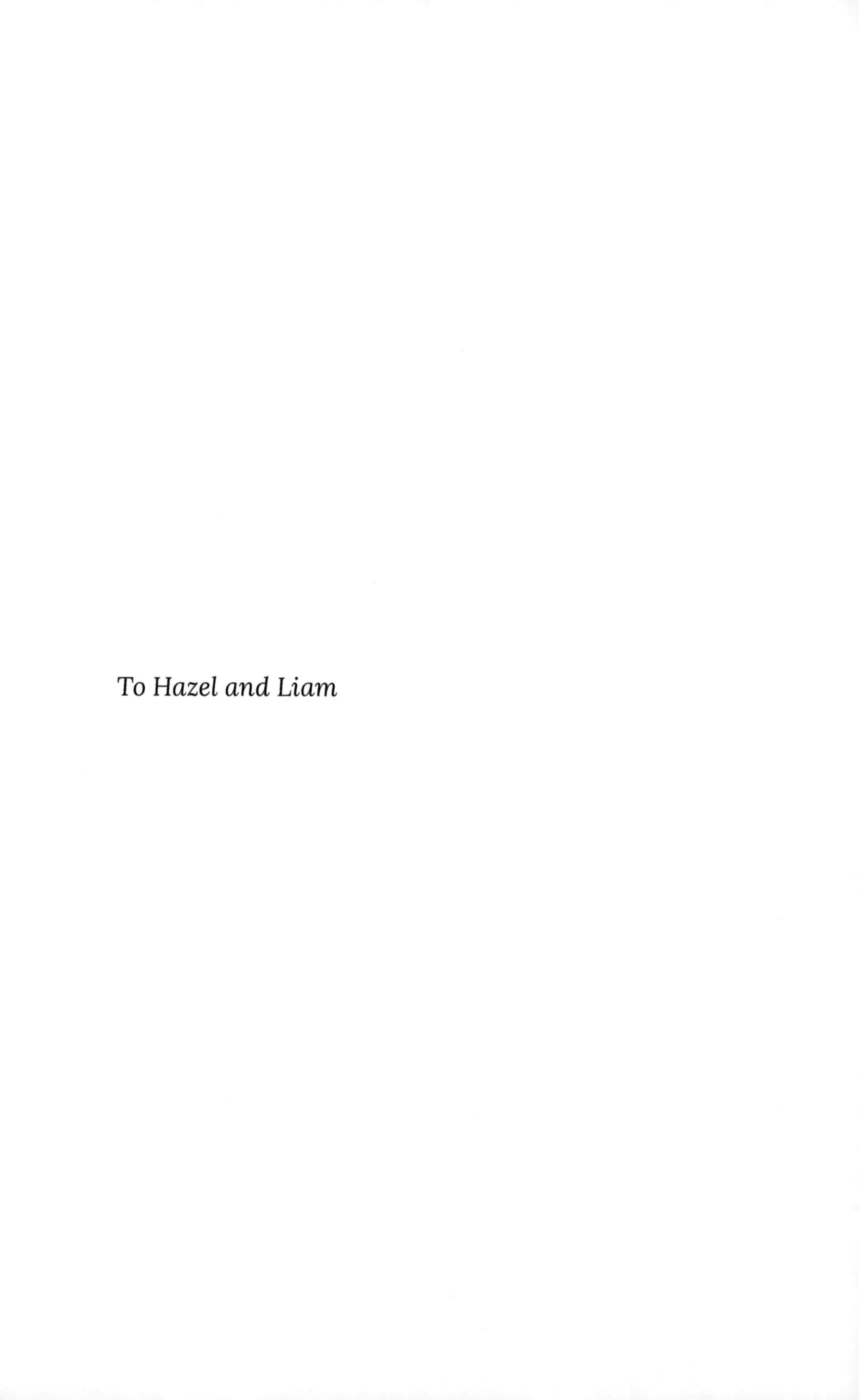

To Hazel and Liam

TABLE OF CONTENTS

WHERE ARE YOU NOW?

I sit alone to contemplate
the workings of a muse.
Yet the pages still seem blank,
I wonder what's the use.
Dante wrote of hell and fire,
and Tennyson his table round.
I cry to find my purpose,
where it can be found.
My soul yearns to speak in power,
and call mankind to hear.
Fingers struggle to write the words,
weaving the strands of wyrd.
Is there some texture, a feeling
I can grasp or touch?
When it dangles on the fingertips,
I've found it and am lost.

PROCESSION OF THE ANTS

Indra sat back in his high-backed throne, swatted at a bothersome fly, and belched. Bored. He stretched his massive body, cracking his knuckles toward the skies, then the great god put his head in his hand, running his thick, meaty fingers through his beard, and looked out from his mountaintop across the fluffy white-topped clouds. Hundreds, no, thousands of years had passed since he last stormed from his abode to engage in a heroic feat of strength. Indra's eyelids fluttered closed, his head bobbing with a sudden rumble in his throat from a midafternoon nap. Yet even as sleep lured him, a faint sound drifted upward from the earth far below. The god stirred, rubbing the sleep from his eyes.

Must be my imagination, he mused sullenly, shifting around in the plush cushions of his seat so he could resume napping. Yet, again that faint sound disturbed him. Indra ground his teeth together. He rose from the throne and thundered down the broad steps to the edge of the mountain, where he leaned out over the great expanse of sky that veils the earth in blue.

Moans and groans of despair filtered up the steep, craggy slopes of Indra's mountain, accompanied by the whispering prayers of supplication, for there was a great sorrow on the earth. Indra's thick, black eyebrows knitted together, and from the prayers he pieced together the dilemma confronting the people who dwelt along the usually muddy banks of the Ganges.

A great demon had rested its massive body along the high crest of the Himalayas, blocking the spring runoff and causing the rivers below to dry up. The people suffered successive generations of droughts where many suffered and starved, unable to plant sufficient crops.

Indra flexed his thick arms and smiled—finally there was a task worthy of his strength. He strode back to his throne, picked up the crackling lightning bolt laying on one of the steps, and reached for his sword belt. He noticed while buckling it around his waist that he had to let it out a notch or two beyond normal. *Remember not to drink so much when this is over*, he mused.

With a freshened step, Indra bounded down the mountain and alighted on the snow-covered crest of the Himalayas. Through the frosty vapor of his own breath, Indra saw the demon for the first time. The creature's immense serpent body lay stretched from the headwaters of the Indus in the west to the foothills of the mountain range in the east, its scales shimmering under a crystal-blue layer of ice and weather. Its terrible claws dug into those foothills, gouging deep furrows and rending underlying stone, the very bones of the earth.

Hefting the lightning bolt, Indra trekked through the miles of snow to the creature's head. Still huffing from his hike, Indra squared his shoulders and, with the voice of thunder, called a challenge. The demon raised its head high up into the sky and looked down at the god, open jaws dripping foul saliva in sizzling drops. Yellow eyes surveyed Indra's stature, then the demon bellowed out a laugh that whipped the snow into a blizzard, blinding Indra in the process amid the swirling white.

"What little godling is this?" Vitra cackled with mirth. "Do you really think you can dislodge me from my home?"

Indra rubbed his chin, his eyes defiant as the distant echo of thunder. "Yes," he replied, "I do believe that to be the likely outcome."

The demon laughed again. "Never, in the millions and millions of years since the earth was brought forth by the power of Brahma the Creator, has there been a puny godling as bold as you. This very day shall Vitra crush you with great pleasure!"

Indra let loose a toothy smile. Being a god of action, not of flowery words, he heaved his lightning bolt at Vitra's head. The burst of energy raced upward, but the beast moved with a swiftness that belied its immense size. The bolt seared past and crackled into the aether. The demon sucked in storms then spit green acid in a massive volatile stream. Indra leaped aside, the acid sloshing in a hiss that covered the upper mountains for miles. He pulled out his sword and, with all the strength in his immortal arms, thrust the blade through the creature's hide, crunching the scales as he sliced into the yielding gut.

Vitra shrieked in horror, thrashing about to cast the god off. Indra clung on, twisting and pulling on the blade to widen the terrible wound. Great floods of water burst from Vitra's gullet and rushed madly down the mountains into the empty riverbeds below. The beast's head fell to the ground in a puff of pulverized rock and powdered snow.

Indra smeared his brow with the back of his hand and smiled once more. He had broken a sweat!

Before the god returned home, high atop his mountain, prayers of appreciation already filtered up to him. The inhabitants and demigods of the earth expressed gratitude to which they admitted the inability to repay fully. One of the minor gods, a spritely immortal named Vishvarkarma, traveled personally to Indra's mountaintop bearing a petition from all the people of India.

"Oh, mighty Indra," began Vishvarkarma, "we are grateful for your mighty arm, which slew the evil demon Vitra." Indra grinned and let him continue. "To show our devotion we ask that you consider our petition." Indra sucked in his gut and released the buckle on his belt. He nodded to Vishvarkarma. "We know you live atop a mountain with no proper place to house yourself."

Indra looked around. His throne jutted out of the mountain, a mere pedestal atop rough-hewn steps. Nothing more. No palace, no rooms, no walls, no gardens, nothing.

Indra rubbed his nose. *I guess I just haven't gotten around to it yet*, he thought.

Vishvarkarma said, "Let us build you a palace; let us construct an edifice to house the great and heroic Indra."

The thought of a palace appealed to Indra. Nothing spectacular, a few simple rooms would suffice. "Very well," he replied. "You may build me a palace."

Vishvarkarma bowed and flitted away back to the earth.

When the work began, Indra watched the thousands of workers, men and gods alike, carry tons of quarried rock, exotic woods, silks, carpets, garden plants, and blown glass up the side of his mountain. Eventually he grew bored and excused himself to take an extended trip. He found a quiet place to while away the tens and hundreds of years, which passed before the palace was scheduled to be completed. Men worked their entire lives, died, and, sometimes, were reborn to the task of hauling materials up the steep and treacherous slopes.

The palace rose from the mountaintop like a glittering piece of polished alabaster, glistening far above the tops of the highest clouds. When it was completed, Vishvarkarma sought out Indra and discovered the mighty warrior–god lying in the sun, sipping a huge, sloshing goblet of wine.

"Oh, mighty Indra," said the spritely god with a bow, "we have completed a building that will house you in the dignity and glory you deserve. We await your return so that any necessary personal alterations may be accomplished while the labor is still assembled."

Indra arrived at the palace with Vishvarkarma, alighting amidst the thousands of men and gods who beamed with pride at the beauty of the wondrous edifice they now presented to their savior. Indra walked through the gilded gates in awe of the beauty in the courtyard, but it could use another tree here, or there. He caught his breath in wonder as they entered the throne room, all awash in sunlight on the rose-colored marble floors. It could use another tapestry on the south side. Indra clapped his hands with delight in the banquet hall as he surveyed the long, long, straight tables that could comfortably seat over a thousand. It could use a smaller, more intimate room to the other side. On and on, Indra walked through his palace, full of praise for the craftsmanship, all the while pointing out the site for another garden here, or a new room there, or a tower overlooking this particular view, or a new pool to reflect that.

As Indra lay on his new bed that very night, he closed his eyes, satisfied that the alterations would be sufficient. But only after they changed the mattress. It was much too stiff.

The next day, and the next, through the next month, the next year, and the following decade, and into the next century, Indra continually roamed the halls of his palace with Vishvarkarma, pointing out "minor changes" to be accomplished. The god supervised the new construction with tremendous vigor and lay awake at night believing that the previous day's alterations were the last. The size of the palace grew into a sprawling, twisting maze of rooms, halls, closets, courtyards, dining rooms, and towers. Generations of men continued to labor in his service, as did the gods who had originally promised to build the palace.

One day, Vishvarkarma's patience ran thin. He had walked and walked the miles of corridors with Indra, watching old men fulfill their dharmas and die on the slopes of the mountain in Indra's service—only to be replaced with fresh young men. Enough was enough. However, Vishvarkarma couldn't bear the thought of facing Indra himself. Had he not been the one to petition him in the first place? Frantic to find a solution, the god decided to seek an audience with the great god Vishnu, the Preserver, and place the problem at his mercy.

With the speed of a lightning bolt, Vishvarkarma shot upward to the higher regions where Vishnu dwelt among the heavenly bodies of stars and planets. With his head bowed, he entered Vishnu's audience chamber and addressed a petitioned to him.

"Oh, great Vishnu," he said humbly as he knelt at the god's feet, "for nearly a thousand years we have been laboring to complete the task of building a palace for Indra..."

Vishnu leaned forward in his throne to listen to the sobbing demigod as he related the entire tale to him. At the conclusion, he placed a firm hand on Vishvarkarma's head.

"Fear not, for you have completed your responsibilities." With those words, Vishnu rose from his hallowed throne and wrapped himself in his cloak, disappearing in a twinkle of light.

The following day, while Indra sat on his velvet-covered throne contemplating changes in a new wing of kitchens, there was a muffled knock at the front gate. A young boy of about ten entered and stood with cowed eyes before the god.

"Oh mighty Indra," the boy said in a timid voice. "My family has spoken of the wonders of your palace for generations, telling me since I was quite young that it expands, as does your glory. They also say it is larger than any palace the previous Indras have built." Indra perked up and lost his thoughts at the boy's praise. "Oh, mighty one, may it please thee to show me this palace of palaces?"

Indra was taken with the boy's pleasantries and consented to show him through every nook and cranny. The pair spent the entire day exploring a small fraction of the entire complex.

As the sun began to set, Indra showed the boy back to the front gate and said, "Come back on the morrow and I shall show you more of my home." Indra looked up over the gate and saw a mason putting a gem in one of the capstones, not quite where it should be. After instructing him on the proper placement, the god opened the gate to let the boy through.

At the moment the portal parted, Indra stepped back aghast. Into his palace paraded a single-file column of ants, one after another. He looked as far as he could, but the column appeared to be endless with relentlessly marching insects. When he finally turned back to the boy, Indra saw through the young human flesh at the true identity of his guest.

"Vishnu? What is this?" he asked.

Vishnu shrugged and said, "Nothing more than other Indras, who in previous lives built their palaces too large."

Indra's jaw dropped.

Then he turned and, waving his arms frantically, ran back into the palace, shouting at the top of his thunderous lungs for the workers to stop what they were doing immediately.

ANTONY, HE GOES
NOT ALONE—

"The blade goes there,"
I said, "a little higher up
beneath the very last rib."
Point pressed against my breast
my hand trembled;
strange, how it that slew so many
fears yet to take one more.
She steadied my fingers,
eyes a blur of stinging tears,
for beyond him lay
the final battlefield.
Proud, the legions of the East once rode,
beneath the standard of Queen and Rome,
broken it now lay,
splintered metal and bone;
carrion birds above ride
tepid currents of the air.
Slight, my hand jolted,
the prick into skin, and I
knew then reality set in, for
beads of sweat dot my hands,
my knuckles whiten around the hilt.
"Tell all," I choked.
"Antony dies proudly this day,
stalwart of Caesar, citizen of Rome,

proud Triumvir,
with nary a throne to my name.
Tell them I'll rot in Pluto's dark home,
than see Octavian rule the world..."
No more thought,
I threw myself forward—
the hilt hit the ground
to thrust the hot steel
b'tween bruised ribs and
into chilled flesh,
cold even on Egypt's arid sands,
and hungrily soaking my blackening blood.
The snake's lethal kiss
sends her to torment him still.

THE CRY OF THE HUNT

The shrilly shrieking horn
echoes through the throng
of leafless shadow trees,
and cries across the rolling
drifting mists of morn.

The quarry stumbles, falters,
and slows its weary pace,
knowing deep within
even death refuses end
to this hellish chase.

Hounds bray, breaking brush,
hurl their sleek forms ahead,
along the warm, fresh track.
Oh, how they howl, these
terrible harbingers of death.

Followed by the great
hair-horned huntsman.
Atop his spike-wheeled chariot,
he scans the forest gloom,
red eyes agleam.

Pleasure is the hunt which
hazes his misty breath.
Again, the bronze horn raising
to thin and pale lips.

The note shrieks,
echoes above sightless trees.

Around the grey-tipped spear
flexes a cruel iron hand.
Crimson, red turns to black
and fades into grey.

He laughs,
and does not care.

A heartless noise
the hounds let loose,
the huntsman to make aware,
and hold the terrible beasts at bay
with a stern command.

He thunders from chariot,
echoing to the ground,
and silent, piercing,
stands before ancient
gnarled limbs.

Above on outstretched branch
curls the shapeless form.
Black against the predawn grey;
it trembles, deathly cold.

Fighting still, the biting chill
it clings tighter to the bark.
The quarry looks 'pon
that ancient horrid face,
and finds in mind a prayer of youth
to Mother Mary
commend my soul,
for after death
hither shall I go.

The huntsman laughed,
a wretched sound.
Call to your gods, for
where are they now?
Silent, distant, they've no power here.

Many a millennia, I've hunted this isle
and will for a millennium more.

They fear my hunt from
sweet Gwynedd's wood
to the rocks off Cornwall.
And so shall you, my friend,
in the hole of Annwyn's gloom.

The mortal cried
to silent god once more, and
yowled in despair as the
cruelly barbed spear tore
living, beating heart.

The huntsman called his hounds to heel,
the sun burst cross Albion's sky.
Fresh, what he came for
the hunt once more complete.

The sun's bright rays alone
to illuminate,
warm rubied blood, turning black,
then grey,
and somewhere in Annwyn's
sinister hell,
a screaming soul is put
away.

THE LOST SPELL

Thondric stomped around and around the dimly lit chamber. His slender body shook with anger, which was punctuated by the staccato thump of his booted feet on the floor. His silken cloak hung from his shoulders and whispered about his ankles, lending him a spectral look that spoke to his profession as a mage, a magicker, and a wizard. His scholarly eyes squinted at the slanted sunlight. He raised a hand to filter the light.

Imagine the audacity of some creatures, he thought, *and this one was a human!* This enraged him all the more—a man thinking to do something clever. Not in all his six hundred years of professional life had anyone dared such a stunt, to actually break into his study and steal a spell. The thought of it made him tear at the silvery locks on his head. Not just any spell, mind you—only the single most important spell ever concocted, the absolutely finest product of 212 years of spell crafting! His long, long sought-after presentation before Oberon's court was in a fortnight. If he did not have the spell, he, the greatest elfin wizard of the age, would be a laughingstock.

Thondric slowed to a stop as a puzzled look crept over his finely boned face. What had that spell been about?

He hadn't entirely forgotten the words, but he couldn't quite remember what it had been for. Funny thing about spells—they tended to slip away from memory with the passage of time, so writing them down helped considerably. This was especially true with major spells, for words and hand signs became increasingly complex to support higher magicks. But now the scarlet, leather-bound volume that had contained the incantation was gone. Nothing more than its dusty outline remained, and even this had faded over the time that had passed since it had been purloined. The fact that Thondric had not noticed it missing until now did nothing to ease his wrath.

Shaking dust bunnies from his fingers, Thondric again paced. Such a grand spell—well, what he could recall of it seemed grand enough—was now in the hands of a mere human, a charlatan at best! It could never be fully appreciated by a mortal.

Of all men, there was only one capable of stealing it.

Merlin.

The old rogue, why for a magician, he was the worst kind. The only reason he had gotten the job in the shamble town of Londinium was because old Uther Pendragon giggled and clapped when fire crackled from the mage's fingertips upon demand. Not that Thondric had wanted the job; he wouldn't have been able to bear even a day in the court of the detestable humans, surrounded by poisonous iron implements. Of more complex magicks and spells, the elf was convinced Merlin stole the spell rather than create his own. For the sake of magic and honor, there was but one course of action. Thondric the Elf was going to Londinium to demand the return of his spell.

Amid a pitter-patter of rain that dribbled through the forest, the elf trudged along the path. He pulled his willow-green traveling cloak farther up about his ears, vainly attempting to keep the rain from dripping down his neck. Beneath his cloak he carried a small pack into which he had stuffed a minor spell book accompanied by odd and sundry magic ingredients—all close at hand. In a barbaric world such as medieval Albion, one could not be too careful. Glaring at the weather, Thondric set his course east toward Londinium.

Jingle, clank, clang, jingle—a pots-and-pans, sort-of-musical sound drifted to the elf's ears, quickly followed by the creak of a leather harness, heavy breathing, and a thick slogging in the muck. A horse and rider emerged, towering out of the mist. The man appeared sodden as well, a damp woolen cloak pulled up about his face. Just visible beneath were a clinkety coat of chain mail that was rusted like the first frost of winter on autumn leaves and weathered leather breeches. His cheeks were flushed with the cold, yet he cheerfully whistled a tune between his teeth. The spurs on his heels marked the rider as a knight—the most arrogant, pompous, overbearing group of ruffians in the whole human species!

"Ho there, little man!" said the knight, raising a hand in an innocuous gesture of greeting.

"Little man!" Thondric repeated. Little man, indeed! The elfin magicker didn't stop.

The warrior lightly spurred to a trot. "Wait, please, sir."

Thondric wasn't amused. For three hundred years, he'd not conversed much with humans, let alone visited their world; why would he want to start now?

The knight pulled up his mount in front of the disgruntled elf, stopping him in his tracks. "Sir, I'm sorry if I said anything to offend—"

"Little man, indeed!" retorted the elf. He pulled a hand from beneath his cloak and extended it toward the horse and rider. Power crackled between his fingertips.

The horse shied, rolling its eyes and snorting. The knight struggled to keep it under control to no avail. The beast reared, pawing the air with its hooves and sending glops of muck flying, and deposited the rider, jingling mail and all, into the mud.

"Why, you little wretch!" the knight growled as he scrambled to his feet.

Thondric raised his glowing hand in warning, though he couldn't help but chuckle. Power popped and sizzled in the air, the pungent scent of ozone floating to his nose from the combustion. The knight dropped a hand to the hilt of the sword hanging at his side.

"Call me little man—bah!" said Thondric. "Of all the brash insults—me, a man!"

The knight sketched an awkward bow. "I apologize, sir," he offered. "I should have used better manners to address such a powerful mage. I've little experience in such things."

"Yes, as well you ought. Why, humans have inhabited this world for barely a few thousand years. Yet you act like you're the only ones walking the woods."

"I'm truly sorry," said the knight as he wiped a glop of mud from his face. "I hadn't realized..."

"Indeed! Now if you would please remove yourself from my path—we elves are little inclined to waste time!"

The knight stepped aside.

The power around Thondric's fingers snuffed out, and with a flourish, he thrust his hand back into his cloak. He resumed tromping ahead.

The warrior whistled for his mount, which quickly trotted back. The knight scooped up the dangling reins and set off to catch up with the grumpy elf.

"Please, Sir Wizard, let me provide recompense for the offense. If you need a ride, at least allow me to assist as far as I may."

"Londinium," Thondric hissed. "I'm going to Londinium on the Thames." He didn't exactly understand why he told the knight this, except that the youth did seem a rather friendly sort—for a human, that is. Maybe he had acted a little hastily.

"Oh, so am I, eventually," said the knight. "At least I can take you part of the way."

Thondric noticed the knight's voice appeared to stray to a distant thought for a moment; it pricked his curiosity. Not that he was interested in the affairs of men—he was just curious. And riding, even with a human, was far better than walking, particularly in Albion. The knight didn't seem to be a bad sort, as far as humans go.

"On one condition," the elf said. "You must tell me why you might not reach Londinium."

The knight nodded and pushed a lock of straw-blond hair from his cheek. "I've no wish to bore a powerful wizard with the mundane."

Without another word, the young man placed a muddy boot in a stirrup and swung atop his mount. He reached down, offering a hand to aid his newly acquired companion. Thondric grabbed it and scrambled behind the knight, just in front of a simple white shield strapped across the horse's flank.

Odd, he thought; no insignia was embossed across its surface. Only a knight-errant, a young man of common or lower birth, would bear such a shield. This young man certainly fit that description, Thondric observed—threadbare clothes, worn leather, and rusted armor. The bare shield was part of his rite of passage. Upon receiving his spurs of knighthood, the knight-errant's name was stripped away to be returned with a noble title upon completion of a quest. If the knight died while carrying out that quest, he left this life nameless and forgotten forever. Holy cups, saints' bones, and other interesting artifacts were of great interest at court, and with so many quests in need of completion, many an errant's bones littered lawless Albion of late.

The knight's voice broke into a cheery tune as they trotted through the dripping forest. It sliced through the elf's thoughts like a bread knife. The youth colored the ride by boisterously singing songs brimming with valor, war, and victory. The countryside blurred as the elf dozed, though he continued to listen to the knight's voice. As he drifted, Thondric half decided to help the young man. There was something different about this one, though he was brash and rumpled around the edges. Perhaps the human race was growing to maturity at last? A shame it would be if this lad were left to molder in a nameless grave. Besides, Merlin would be at Londinium entertaining the royalty for quite some time. He could retrieve the spell a little later.

A brisk nip hung in the air and scattered a thin crust of autumn frost across the land. Laboring through the early morning light, the horse heaved great white puffs while its iron-shod hooves crunched through the grass that soon would thaw and give way to the mud beneath. However, the weather wasn't the only thing to transform with the approach of dawn. The knight was no longer the cheery youth—his features had become grim. Today the youth would face the test of his young life.

The narrow track gradually became a broad lane through the barren elm and oak trees. The riders passed bits of armor littering the pitted ground. Battered helmets lay alongside rusting breastplates. Splintered shields hung from limbs of trees that grew more sinister as the knight and elf rode by. Telltale signs of an ogre, Thondric observed. The particular breed infesting this corner of Albion was a nasty bunch that never cleaned up their messes. The pair remained silent as they bounced through the wreckage, though Thondric wrinkled his nose in disgust, his fine elfin sense of smell assailed by the foul air. He recalled that another tendency of ogres, besides leaving garbage about their lairs, was to never bathe. And judging by the smell of things, Thondric decided that it had been more than a few years since this one had dipped even a toe in any form of water.

Decaying bones poked out of the thawing ice—a worm-riddled skull here, a slivered leg bone there. Many a fallen warrior would remain nameless in this place, remembered only as a long-past meal. You see, ogres' stomachs constituted a never-ending pit. If one ingested an entire cow, it would merely serve to entice his enormous appetite to greater depths of gluttony.

Thondric tightly clutched his spell book when the black maw of a cave appeared out of a grey-brown cleft in a hillside: the entrance to the ogre's lair. *Should have put thumb tabs on the pages*, he thought, tracing the edges of the worn pages with his fingers.

The young man reined up his mount and swung off its back.

"You wait here, please, Sir Wizard. I have no desire for you to die," he said.

"So you really haven't had much experience with elven wizards."

"Why no," replied the knight.

"If you really knew us, then you'd realize that my people are great sorcerers, especially in battle." It was a little white lie, but it was worth the flicker of a smile that turned the knight's lips up. The man loosed his shield from the saddle. Upon sliding his arm into the straps on the back, the knight straightened his broad shoulders and sucked the fetid air between his clenched teeth.

"Ogre! Come forth!"

The knight waited, his fingers tapping on the hilt of his sword. But the only response was silence.

"Hear me, vile creature! Come forth!" he shouted again. When there was still no reply, the knight turned to Thondric, a puzzled look on his face. Perhaps ogres didn't respond to noble challenges. Then again...

Rumbling shook the ground, nearby rocks chattering and clattering. When the creature thrust its ugly snout from the cave's shadows, the elf's insides fluttered. The bloated man-like face leered at the intruders, exposing jagged, rotten teeth. What followed was its hulking body girded about with a soiled loincloth. From the ogre's meaty fist swung a huge, knotted club.

"A puny man! You come to fight me?" the beast bellowed. "Hungry now—I eat you both!"

"Yes, come fight, vile creature!" The knight hauled his sword from the scabbard at his side. "By all that's holy, I'll end your pillaging of fair Albion!"

A bit bold, Thondric thought, *but if it helps his confidence...*

The ogre pounded the ground with its club and then rushed forward. The knight launched himself to meet the attack, shouting oaths of defiance. Warrior clashed against ogre in midstride. His blade bounced off thick ogre hide. The beast replied with its club, splintering the knight's shield. The warrior staggered. Then with a monstrous swing of the club, the ogre caught him with a crushing blow to the chest, the impact hurling the knight through the air.

Thondric whispered a few words, his hand extended before him as the power flashed between his fingers. A sizzling white ball shot through the air and exploded against the ogre's chest. The beast snorted, brushing away the lingering remnants of the spell as the knight dragged himself from the ground.

"Saint Michael's bones," the knight growled, shaking the cobwebs from his head. He staggered to his feet and attacked again.

Thondric nervously rifled through his spell book; he found it hard to concentrate with all the clatter of wood and metal. If only the two combatants could be quiet for a moment—just a moment. The elf peeked up from the page to see the ogre lift the knight over its head like a rag doll. He raced through the pages until he finally found the desired spell. The contents of his pack tumbled to the ground as he searched for the necessary ingredients. A small leafy sprig lay in the muck alongside a stub of beeswax candle. He grabbed the candle with one hand, passing the other over the dried leaves while speaking aloud the required words.

The magic power arched from his fingers and ignited the plant in a brilliant flash.

POOF!

A small kitten appeared.

The elf stomped his foot in frustration. Well, catnip was a mistake.

From the corner of his eye, he saw the shards of the knight's sword bouncing off the ogre's hide. Into the backpack went the kitten, out came another bloom, and he tried once more. This time a large black war hound appeared, standing shoulder to shoulder with the knight's charger. Dogwood. Its eyes glowed wildly, red tongue lolling out of the side of its mouth. With the beastly monster chomping at the knight's head, Thondric commanded the attack. Without hesitation, the war hound sprang into the fray. Slashing, magical teeth gashed the ogre, the hound seeking a hold around its throat. The ogre tossed the knight, and its meaty fists struck back at the hound. But Thondric ignored this and rushed to the knight's side.

"Come on, come on," urged Thondric.

The warrior struggled to his feet.

"Come on—that dog won't last long getting beaten like that!" Even now, the ogre's clenched fists battered the hound. But it continued to attack, its teeth penetrating the thick ogre skin and drawing beads of dark blood.

Foul blackness engulfed them when man and elf plunged into the cave. Thondric muttered a word and crackling light engulfed his hand, illuminating the pathway. They picked their way through the muck and slime, the long-legged man at times tugging his companion along when the elf stumbled. Through the gloom they continued until light glowed in the distance, growing brighter as they trudged forward. Eventually they tumbled into the sunlight and onto a verdant green knoll that was surrounded by rugged hills and thick forest. The knight wiped grimy sweat from his face and surveyed below them. There was a lake covered by a thin layer of swirling mist. At the beach lay a rickety rowboat.

"This, my friend, is where we part company," the knight said. "Now I must earn my name and spurs alone."

The warrior strode toward the boat.

"Hurry, Sir Knight. That ogre won't wait all day before giving chase!" Thondric found a nearby rock to squat on. He watched the youth push the boat from the sand into the water. The knight clambered aboard and settled to the oars. With repeated heaving of the oars, he propelled the craft across the water to the center of the lake, the water beneath still obscured from the elf's view by the mist that lay upon the surface. The knight allowed the boat to drift and lifted the oars from the locks. Even at a distance, the elf perceived power, intense power, radiating from the watery depths. Each wave made his body tremble. There were serious magicks here, probably some of the mightiest he'd ever encountered. Certainly this was sorcery of a high order. Yet this magic had a familiar feeling to it that the elf could not place.

The surface of the water began to bubble and break into rollicking waves that rippled through the mist. The knight grabbed the boat's rail and then slowly stood. Vapors blanketing the water peeled back, exposing the grey liquid beneath. Then the waves parted with a splash, and a glistening blade thrust into the air. Water rushed down the blood channel, and then streamlets continued running past the exquisitely jeweled cross guard and down the slender, pale hands and arms of an elfin woman.

Thondric jumped to his feet for a better look.

The sorceress beckoned the knight with a nod. The youth took a visible breath before stepping from the boat onto the quivering water. Sheathed in English wool and iron, he towered over the woman yet looked upon her as if enwrapped in a faerie dream. She lowered the blade from over her head and placed it into the knight's hands. White power crackled from the enchanted air and came to rest at the tip of the glistening sword. That light shot down the blade to flame around the knight's hands. He did not cry out in pain or discomfort, for the sword had accepted him.

The knight gingerly touched the blade with trembling fingers before grasping the hilt and thrusting the mystic sword over his head. He cried out and swung the weapon, reflecting myriad rainbows from its polished surface.

Thondric clapped his hands at the spectacular display. Yet all too soon, the knight sheathed the sword in the empty scabbard at his side. With a bow, he kissed the lady's hand and then walked back to the boat. He didn't look back at the sound of water gurgling when the sorceress slipped once again beneath the waves.

When the bow of the boat finally grated the beach, the enraged beast shredded the enchanted vision. The ogre rushed from the cave into the sunlight. It beat titanic fists against its bloody, torn chest. With a bestial roar, it hurled itself toward the object of its anger—the lone knight.

The knight hauled the sword from its scabbard and stepped forward to meet the onslaught.

Thondric shrank back when the creature screamed, for the blade wetted itself in black blood. The ogre recoiled in fear, no longer impervious to the knight's spirited assault. Blood spattered the sand, and the lake's hungry waves lapped into crimson foam. With a cry to his god and a powerful sweeping cut, the knight clove through bone and muscle, disemboweling the beast. It fell to its knees, desperately clutching at its entrails, and then toppled face into the sand.

The knight sank to a knee, clutching the sword to his chest. He bowed his head, frozen in the semblance of a grateful pilgrim.

Thondric took a step down the hill, but a hand caught his shoulder. The elf looked up into the lean, white-bearded face of an elderly human. Devilish mirth flickered in clear-blue eyes, and Thondric recognized the object of his own quest, Merlin, the mage of Uther Pendragon.

Merlin raised a finger to his lips nearly hidden behind that thicket of beard. "I know, old friend. I owe you an explanation. But without your spell none of this would have happened."

Thondric had a biting retort already prepared for this moment, yet he bit his tongue. There was a new feel in the air.

Merlin continued. "Uther lies wasting from illness, leaving the kingdom in turmoil, for there is no heir apparent. This young man"—Merlin pointed to the knight-errant—"Arthur by name, is Uther's son and rightful heir to the throne. He has now earned his name and his sword. Your spell alone was strong enough to bind the power of light into the steel, tempering the union in the tears of a god. Thus armed, he can lay claim to the throne and bring peace to this land."

Thondric furrowed his brows. The sword. The spell. *His* spell.

This was the child whose birth had been heralded to the faerie realms seventeen years ago and celebrated for a year and a day. Thondric had thought it foolish at the time, honoring a human event with such festivities. Yet he himself had taken part in the delegation sent to fair Y'graine after the child's birth to present elven gifts.

Merlin clapped Thondric on the shoulder. "And of course, you've seen my colleague, the Lady of the Lake. You created a spell so powerful it took two of us to cast it. Through your incantation, steel has come to life—a life devoted to stopping the flood of chaos threatening Albion—a life that will be praised in song and legend for centuries. When people think of Arthur, they will also recall his sword, Excalibur."

Trying to look indignant for the entire inconvenience, Thondric muttered, "Why didn't you ask me? Oh, you humans!"

"My friend," Merlin said with a sly grin, "when I saw your spell, I knew it to be a magical masterpiece. Now that you've seen what your spell can do, I know you won't begrudge an old friend for a little thievery."

"Humpf." Thondric was not yet ready to let him off the hook so easily. "I'll have that spell back now, if you please, Merlin."

The human suddenly looked sheepish beneath his wild eyebrows. "Oh, well...You see, um...Now, Thondric, don't get angry..."

"What happened to my spell?"

Merlin planted his staff defiantly in the ground. "It was consumed by the casting."

"Amateurs!" Thondric stomped his feet in sheer frustration. "That was over two hundred years of work!"

"Oh, yes, we could tell. But, you see, it *was* slightly unstable."

The elf puffed his cheeks out and narrowed his eyes. "Harrumph," he grumbled. "You just can't trust humans!"

"Besides, a sporting adventure has brought a bit of color to your cheeks. Well, all's well that ends well, yes? Farewell, Thondric!"

The magician waved a hand over the elf. In a twinkle, Thondric crossed the gulf between the planes and was once again standing beside his desk. To his left a bare spot on his shelf, where used to reside a scarlet leather volume, yet taunted him.

Oberon would have fun at his expense over this—for centuries. He could hear the laughter even now. On the other hand, a young man had come into his own and would lead his people out of darkness into the light of wisdom and virtue.

For that, he decided, he could bear the joke.

FORGING

Thousands of precious drops all spilt
the cool, thick liquid to temper,
black gouts of steam, floating
stinking putrid fumes—
hand-beaten steel hardening,
swimming in thickening blood.
They say dwarves took the metal,
dark in its natural state
and beat from the iron—
steel hot.
The bellows fanned the flames
turning the metal white,
all hell, all hell broke loose
at the singing site.
They bled a god for the fluid
to temper the steel strong.
Swirling in the bloody clots
it stirred and burst forth in song.

Redder than a newborn babe,

ebony black the blade, the bane of demons

and of men

wicked verse did sing:

"Champions come

and champions go

hie the way of mortal flesh.

Great rivers of blood,

I shall reap,

blowing in the eternal winds.

Forever in the endless cycle

scream death, howl in the night

the remorse, oh champion,

of the day that I was found."

WHAT'S IN A NAME?

Thunderer's shattered peak loomed high above the dusty Garoc plains, that long-ago battlefield of gods and demons. An enormous shattered spike of rock and debris was all that remained of the once great mountain range that in ages past had spanned the length of Western Earthland. Thunderer's granite siblings lay like the broken ribs of a wasted carcass, scattered across Garoc's vast brown landscape. Yet still, Thunderer's forbidding spire reached high enough to scrape the bellies of the stray clouds that dared leap over it. And from its still-formidable heights rose columns of dark vapor streaming into the expanse of blue.

Directly above, the midday sun relentlessly shot blistering barbs of light on six weary and dust-caked elves tramping up the steep mountain track. Waves of phantom heat rose off the dark rocks. One of their number, a willowy elf clad in the faded green of a Royal Scout with an officer's sash girded about his waist, scrambled lithely up a boulder to gauge their progress. He raised his hand, signaling the band to halt. Behind him, the elves peeled sweat-slickened packs from their bodies and collapsed in exhausted heaps. Some shook their canteens, listening for a rattle from inside. Once unstoppered, the canteens' trickles of stale water tantalized their parched, grumbling lips, for the last stream the company had happened upon had been fouled.

After many long months, the whittled-down band finally approached their destination—the lair of the wyrm. This band no longer quested at full strength, for each step of the journey had been paid in blood by the members of the company left behind in scattered graves along the way, crude markers etched on wood and stone silently bearing witness to those sacrifices. These remaining rangers were a ragtag bunch. The remnants of once splendid uniforms hung from their bodies—now patched and stained by the innumerable leagues separating them from their home in the east. Today they jockeyed for position against the broken stone, pressing their bodies into the sparse shade and gnawing hungrily on the last of their provisions.

Vondrall crouched atop the rock and watched the others for a moment. Gunolf, the oldest of the group, circulated among the others, reminding each of them, with a shake of his gnarled fingers and a crackling voice, to reserve the precious water in their flasks. They complied with minimal grumbling. Demetrai, a slender ranger with long locks tied into a single braid down his back, lifted a mock toast to Gunolf's health, then dramatically swigged his few drops. Jan, a tangle-headed youth, and Twill, a disheveled scholarly sort, dropped with their packs against a rock and stretched out next to them. Vondrall knew that more than a few moments in the same spot and their knucklebones would clatter at the base of the rock. The two had won and lost each other's clothes so many times during the journey that the wagers had become a running joke with all their comrades. And as always, the soldier Valerian remained standing, ever the sentinel, armed with swords, daggers, and a war hammer strapped to his slender body. These were those who remained from the company that began the quest from Elvin Home, the land of the Folk.

And he?

Well, Vondrall began the journey as Command Fourth, a junior officer, when the king had requisitioned rangers from the Milvin Eagles for this mission—the troop snatched away from the battalion preparations for a winter rotation on the Solorent border monitoring military movements of the human kingdom. All told, thirty-five rangers, each skilled in long-range expeditions and survival, left their comrades behind following the fortnight of celebrations marking the king's nuptials. Vondrall, barely ninety-three years of age, had been advanced from the ranks just days before as the Command Fourth. And from the day they set out from Elvin Home, orcs, goblins, and humans had hunted the troop the length of the continent until now there were but six. And with the death of each officer, honor required the mission to continue. Through deep and dangerous forests, bramble-choked warrens, and ice-covered mountain passes, they had pushed on. And every time an officer fell, the carefully guarded mission lore was passed to the next officer in the line of command until finally that information had been entrusted to Vondrall.

A shout of alarm interrupted his thoughts, and he scrambled to his feet.

"Look! Look over there!" Valerian called, pointing down the serpentine course through the rocks.

Vondrall shaded his eyes and looked back across the lower slope. In the distance, brightly colored specks floated like darting insects among the rocks, accompanied by an occasional silvery flash of light.

"Probably wraiths or something," Demetrai growled, scratching at his ears. The elf continued grumbling as he tugged off his battered boots, shaking pebbles out of them.

Vondrall reached into his pouch, fumbled around the assorted contents, then pulled out a set of retractable binoculars. With a click and snap, the device popped open. He raised the viewer to his almandine eyes, swept the tube in the direction of the movement, and focused the powerful lenses. After the barest moment, he shoved the binoculars back into the pouch and sprang down, shouting for the company to return to order. They scrambled to their feet, dragging their packs after their leader in a tumble of confusion.

Gunolf shouldered his way to Vondrall's side and grabbed him by the arm.

"Whoa, just slow down there," he said, twisting a finger nervously in his tangled silver-and-grey beard.

"No time!" the younger elf huffed, his ears burning red.

"What? Why?"

Vondrall skidded to a halt, giving the rest of the band a chance to form up around him. His hand rose to the flat, thick hunk of dried dragon's scale that hung about his neck—entrusted to him by the now long-dead Command Second. "An armored column. Mounted and armed to the teeth! The banner of Santrop, king of Solorent, leads them." He squinted into the distance. "Looks like they'll cross our path near the summit."

Gunolf whistled. Just a hundred years of nervous peace had passed since Gerilian the Grim, king of Solorent, had carved a bloody trail to the very gates of El-vin Home. Puckered scars seamed Gunolf's face from the violent battles he had fought against that human killer. "Didn't know the old boy's out and about these days, let alone on his way up Thunderer." He chuckled in an attempt to raise everyone's spirits. Santrop, the current king, was a pampered fop who had inherited the throne from his father, who was Gerilian's grand-son.

"Probably not the fat bastard himself," Vondrall not-ed. "He hasn't been seen outside the palace in over a decade."

The rest of the company whispered, for there could only be one man in all Solorent, and all Earthland for that matter, intrepid enough to ascend Thunderer and wrest treasure from the serpent within.

"Well, then"—Gunolf chuckled—"we'd best get mov-ing if we're going to beat them to the top!"

"Maybe we don't have to race," Vondrall said. *Perhaps the humans would act in their own self-interest with the right offer.* Besides, the trinket the elves sought was insignificant compared to the mounds of treasure the humans would bear back to their king if success-ful. And surely the beast would be more impressed during negotiations with a company of knights at his back, rather than just this band of threadbare rangers.

"Surely you don't mean..." Valerian began. But a look from Gunolf cut him off.

Vondrall waved the troop across the slopes toward the colorful, arrogant banners of men.

"Column, halt!"

The command rippled back through the line of horsemen that snaked up the broken track leading to the summit. Gilded trumpets blasted crisp, lively signals through the air, but with no forward motion, the scarlet-and-gold banners sagged in the stagnant air. An outrider spurred his tired mount along the column toward the scarlet-plumed command officers riding beneath the banners. Among them, Sir Derring von Bompus slouched in his saddle and, with a meaty hand raised to blot out the sun, squinted against the glare. Sweat ran from his brow and into his eyes, causing him to blink at the nuisance. *Delays, delays,* he thought. The outrider drew alongside the arch knight and saluted with a thump of his mailed fist on his breastplate. Von Bompus nodded back.

"Well?" he demanded.

"Elves, sir," the man reported. "A group of very dirty elves. Their leader requested an audience."

Von Bompus smirked. "Very well. Tell them they may speak with the envoy of Santrop of Solorent."

The trooper rode back the way he came, a squad of horsemen peeling off and pounding along in his wake. A short time later, the troopers escorted the elves back toward von Bompus's position. Even at a distance, he quickly noted their appearance—as would any proper soldier. What were once fine uniforms now hung from their bodies in tattered rags. Their leader, a beardless stripling with long silvery locks curling about his shoulders, saluted the arch knight with a stiff bow. While tall for an elf, he stood no more than average height for a human, his once smart scout uniform now stained, torn, and patched even worse than those of his companions. But his equipment appeared meticulously tended to, and his kit included exotic weaponry that could only have been crafted in the forges of the Folk.

The elf raised a hand, then said, "Sir Derring von Bompus, your name is known in Elvin Home, and we hail you."

The cue for which the royal herald had remained well prepared was given. He flicked his horse's flanks with silver spurs and rode forward from the assembled cavalry. Brushed blond hair hung limply about his hawkish, sunburned face, and a haughty grin turned up the corners of his lips. The man was a riot of colors, from his yellow calfskin boots to his orange silken hose and brightly colored livery.

"Elves of Elvin Home," he bellowed. "I present to you Sir Derring von Bompus, Royal Arch Knight of the Garter, Grand Marshal of the Neldon Order, Master of the Southern Frontier, and Twenty-Fifth Duke of the Gortrim March. Sir Derring von Bompus, the Commander of the Sixth, Twentieth, and Thirty-First Mounted Red Hawks, Warrant General to the First and Ninth Legions posted in Ansalon, and Envoy to the Mercenary Battalions in Quintonestum, Beverelok, and Waterock. Sir Derring von Bompus, Holder of the Royal Signet Meltalik, the seal of King Santrop, also Charter Holder of the Free Fiefs in the Royal Demesne of Sharl and the Dispenser of Pardons on behalf of the Grand Council. Sir Derring von Bompus, victorious at the Battle of Karnak, Humbler of the Pretender at the bloody Battle of Goram Torak, where he..." On and on the man droned, transforming the arch knight's greatest battles into a glorified stream of names and titles.

The elves stirred restlessly, and even Vondrall shook one of his legs to keep it from falling asleep.

Eventually the courtier's speech lumbered to an end. Then, with a curt nod to the elves, he bowed in the saddle to his lord and rode back into the column. The arch knight glared down his pudgy nose at the disheveled elfin band. A stream of sweat rolled off his chin into the depths of his potbellied plate armor.

"Well," he demanded, "what favor have you come to beg of me?"

"We've come to ask nothing, most noble sir, but rather to offer our services in your expedition," Vondrall replied.

Von Bompus raised an eyebrow. "Services? I don't remember requesting aid from Elvin Home. How could you possibly help me?"

"We hail from the court of Cailex the Twenty-Third. We bring capabilities of both arms and sorcery."

"Special mission, indeed," Von Bompus snorted. "Why, you're what's left of Cailex's folly!"

The points on the elf's ears deepened red.

"We're an expeditionary ranger unit of the Milvin Eagles, sir!"

"Oh, come, elfling." The arch knight's response was brutally blunt. "All Earthland knows of your king's foolish promise to his blushing bride. Anything her heart desired shall be hers, if I recall. So she chose an obscure trinket in a bloody dragon's lair as a test of his troth! If he must make such promises, then dip into the treasury and pay for the best!"

"We don't need greedy bleedin' mercenaries!" Gunolf piped up.

"Be that as it may," von Bompus replied, choosing to ignore the insolence. He waved his hand back across the extended column of cavalry troopers. "But we've been in control for each league through this forsaken land, rather than running like rabbits."

"Such numbers are useful on a battlefield," Vondrall conceded. "But against the evil inside Thunder-er, you'll be no match. No matter how long you throw your men against him, the dragon will prevail. You've need of someone skilled in the subtle arts. We can provide that assistance. In exchange, we only desire the Orb of Solomnai."

"You think me fool enough to journey without magical tools of my own?" von Bompus snickered. The arch knight pulled a small, flat disc from his belt pouch. "Not only do I have the requisite piece of drag-on's scale, but I also know the beast's name."

The elf shook his head in disbelief. "No human magicker holds that secret—no matter how much you paid him!"

Von Bompus leaned forward and stared at Vondrall with piercing grey eyes. He raised a meaty finger to the side of his nose and smiled wryly. "And no human magicker has! I was there when the great wizard Cambrai wrested the name from the demon's own lips! So be gone. Run back to hide in Elvin Hole, for I, and I alone, shall best the creature! For I am Sir Derring von Bompus, arch knight of Solorent!"

He dismissed the elves with a wave, then clapped his spurs against his steed's ribs. The elves shuffled aside as the entire company of knights, squires, and baggage carriers lurched to follow their leader.

"The fool," Gunolf said once they had passed, swinging his pack over a shoulder and chuckling. "You tried talking sense to him. If he thinks he has the name, so be it. At least we have it right from Soren's lips. And there's a magicker who knows what he's talking about."

Vondrall spat dust from the passage of von Bompus's troopers, but his mouth remained gritty. "We continue as planned. And we take what we need."

As the day progressed, the terrain grew more difficult with each step. Even so, the elves kept pace with von Bompus's cavalry, which was obliged to scratch for each foothold in the loose rock. By the time the elves had reached Thunderer's jutting summit, the humans had fallen hours behind them. Near that peak of fractured stone, a sulfurous stream meandered from ice that had accumulated in the deep crevices. After long hours tromping through ice and slush while the sun fell toward the distant western horizon, the band stumbled toward an immense hole in the mountain. A brimstone stench wafted from within.

"Welcome to the pit," Gunolf hissed.

Vondrall placed a hand on the cool, broken stone of the hole. "Feel the magic?"

Gunolf nodded. "Frayed ends of a very old detection spell. The trigger's probably farther down the tunnel."

Vondrall squinted into the darkness.

"Hold up!" Gunolf whispered sternly. "Here it is right here."

Vondrall froze. "Here?"

"Almost…" Gunolf gingerly stepped forward, his keen eyes peeling back the darkness along the rough-hewn walls. "There," he said with a satisfied tone. "There it is."

Amid the shadows, ancient serpentine runes crouched like scarlet vipers.

Gunolf took a step back, then conferred with Twill and Demetrai.

"Old—very, very old magic indeed," Twill muttered, rubbing at his own nose and squinting at the runes. "From before the formation of the four kingdoms."

"Looks like Elder Corendellian script to me—from the First Dynasty," Demetrai postulated.

"Well, we aren't going through without tippin' the old bugger off," Vondrall noted.

Jan slithered out of his pack straps, then fished around inside the pack. He pulled out his own set of binoculars and stepped away from the entrance to survey the frosty rock above.

Vondrall sagged against the corridor wall, reaching into a pocket in his dusty trousers and pulling out a crumpled piece of parchment—a crude, hand-drawn map. Smoothing out the wrinkles, he traced the route up Thunderer with his finger. This immense hole appeared to be the only entrance to the lair.

"I'd give my eyes and beard for another way in," Gunolf sputtered.

"Start shavin'." Jan chuckled, passing his binoculars off to Vondrall and directing him with his finger along a line of sight to the west. A plume of smoke drifted into the clouds.

Through the lenses, Vondrall spied dark holes in the ice—warm exhaust from deep in the mountain's gut spewing through vents in the ice. "This place is full of holes from the days when liquid rock flowed from the mountain!"

"Just a different boiler," Twill said and smiled.

Gunolf pointed a finger at Jan. "Be that as it may— I'm not shavin' until we know where this hole of yours goes!"

"Save me a whisker," Demetrai snickered.

Six exhausted elves pulled ropes and spikes from their packs. Vondrall, already bent over the map, plotted their course up the broken rock. Then they set off toward the nearest grey-misted column venting its vaporous trail into the sky.

The sound of mallets striking iron spikes echoed quickly into the expansive sky as the elves utilized ropes and carbineers with the spikes to crawl across the sheer rock. Far beneath them, as the last light retreated over the world's edge, the first of the human cavalry appeared before the dragon's lair. Those troopers quickly deployed into pickets while squires began unloading gear amid the deepening shadows.

But Sir Derring von Bompus remained in his saddle, surveying both the great cavern and the column of troopers stumbling up the treacherous track. He signaled a squire to take his steed's reins, then swung his bulk from the saddle. The night wind stirred from the glaciers clinging to Thunderer's heights, its chilled touch welcome after the endless days of toiling beneath the merciless sun. He stretched his toes in his boots, then strode toward the darkened cave, a squire scurrying behind him bearing aloft a newly lit torch. He brushed the youth away with a gesture.

Vapor washed over his face, causing his nose to twitch and his eyes to water—that stench of burned rock would accompany them into the belly of the mountain. Before him in the gloom, points of light scattered along a crumbling arch. When he approached, the lights flared, stealing his night vision for a moment. From the blur, an illuminated script appeared in the ancient rock, writing that curled and squirmed as if alive. Von Bompus traced the script with a gloved finger, causing the light to turn from golden to crimson.

The arch knight drew his hand back and rubbed at his chin. The serpent had been warned of their arrival; of this he was sure. But no matter—for even this great beast would fall.

Vondrall tested the rope that extended below into the abyss, then swung his feet over the jagged edge. In a moment his keen eyesight adjusted to the stygian darkness, allowing him to cling to the rock immediately at hand, though beneath his boots he saw nothing but the deepest pitch. He launched over the edge into what would be a very long descent into the mountain's heart.

Hand under hand . . . hand under hand. Down the rope he descended for what felt like hours. But he continued downward, counting to himself each movement of his hands to gauge the remaining length of rope. But before testing the end, his feet brushed a slope. He slid down the stone into a channel etched in the rock. After regaining his footing, he tugged on the rope to signal the rest of the group. Soon after, a clatter from far above heralded the remaining rangers' descent along that slender path.

The channel, a narrow track smoothed out centuries before by molten rock rushing toward the surface, proved large enough for an elf on hands and knees to wriggle through. Vondrall squirmed and scraped ahead on his belly. Behind him, one by one, the rest of the company followed. By the time the last elf dropped from the rope, Vondrall was well along the channel, buried deep in the massive rock that crushed down on his woodland sensibilities, for he was bred to be a creature of long summer days and warm moonlit nights. He was unable to fathom the centuries the beast had been bound inside this rock. Yet confined it was, and according to the dictates of the Kinrae, it would remain so unless the terms of its imprisonment were broken. However, the sages who had prepared the rangers for this quest had assured them that couldn't happen.

Eventually a pathway opened wide enough for the elves to crawl on hands and knees, then walk upright. Ahead, a yellow speck appeared and grew with each step. The tunnel opened into a narrow path with a volcanic rim much like a castle's crenellations ringing the inside of a dizzyingly immense cavern. Across the ceiling, numberless glowing creatures wriggled wormy bodies in and out of holes in the rock, generating the ethereal glow. As a youth, an itinerant dwarven smithy had regaled Vondrall with tales of such glowworms. But at the time, he had laughed off the idea of underground fireflies. The elf grabbed at the lip of the stone formation and clambered up for a better look.

There in the heart of the mountain, he felt a cold chill rise up his spine.

Far below lay the dragon in a coiled heap of crimson-scaled flesh—its long, narrow head resting between sharp-clawed paws and facing an enormous black portal. At the thought of the dragon stretching up to snatch him, Vondrall's skin crawled. But the dragon didn't move, didn't look up—it just lay with eyes wide open, all the while rumbling in a steady, slow rhythm. Around the portal, a brilliant red light flashed, warning that the wards at the surface had been activated—as Vondrall was already aware.

According to legend, the mountain had served as the beast's lair for centuries prior to Kinrae imprisoning it. Mounds of accumulated wealth from those ages past attested to the beast's greed. The sleeping beast's long body twisted among staggering mounds of glittering gold and silver coins. Other ancient artifacts were scattered across the lair as well. Vondrall pulled out his binoculars and scanned for the item that had compelled the rangers to cross the world. After repeated passes over the hoard, carefully exploring all the shadowed nooks and crannies, a shimmer caught his eye. He refocused the lenses and there, cradled on a moldering velvet pillow, was the Orb of Solomnai—a translucent sphere that looked no bigger than a pala'wa ball, easily cupped in two hands.

Hooves echoed down the long track through the mountain to the portal, announcing the arrival of the humans before Sir Derring von Bompus appeared upon his proud charger. The arch knight's steed pawed at the floor with massive iron-shod hooves, shaking its head. Flecks of sweat and spittle flew into the air. The dragon stirred with a stretching yawn while the rest of the cavalry pushed raggedly into the cavern upon their frightened mounts. From the chaos, the pale courtier was squeezed forward atop his own skittish steed, his skin a pale shade of grey.

"Dragon, t-t-to you is pres-s-sent-ted . . . Sir D-d-derring von Bom—Bompus, Royal Arch Knight of the G-g-arter, Grand M-m-m-arshal of the Neldon Order..." Then his high-pitched voice fell into a nervous cadence when it became apparent he would not be eaten.

As the courtier droned on, Vondrall backed away from the edge and slid down among his men.

"Okay," he said, stripping off his pack and tugging a large sack out of it. "We'll be needing that last coil of rope."

Valerian grabbed the rope, clutching it in his fist. "I'll go," he said gruffly. "You shouldn't. You're the last of the command."

"And you'll be needed if my plan unravels. Get them all out of the mountain and return home." Vondrall thrust out his hand for the rope. "That's my order—obey it!"

Gunolf climbed up onto the edge of the rim. "Hur-ry," he whispered, "before that poor fellow chokes on his own tongue."

Valerian's jaw bulged, but then with an exasperated gasp, he relented.

Jan took the rope from him and tossed it up to Gunolf, who looped it over an outcropping and eased it unnoticed down the inside of the rim until it flopped at the bottom. Vondrall scrambled up, took hold of the rope, and slid over the side.

"Don't forget the spells you have hanging in the nether!" Gunolf hissed after him. "Use them sparingly—there are only a few!"

Derring von Bompus stewed like a poached pickled herring in his heavy parade armor. But at this, his greatest moment, he ignored the discomfort—for this grand expedition would crown his name with eternal glory.

From across the cave, the courtier haltingly recounted the arch knight's prowess at the Battle of Goram Torak, where he'd scattered an orc regiment with but his broken sword and lame horse.

Von Bompus sneezed.

A rumble germinated deep inside the dragon's gullet until it erupted from its toothy mouth. At the noise, the cavalry broke into confusion, except for von Bompus, who retained firm control of his charger. He slapped up his visor, inhaling the steamy vapors that swirled about as one might take in an aromatic perfume.

The dragon cocked its head, its baleful eyes narrowly examining Sir Derring von Bompus.

"Ho there, ancient one!" the arch knight roared.

"You've interrupted my sleep," the dragon snorted. "Why are you here?"

"Surely you must know. I'm here to take your treasure!" The arch knight shifted his rotund body.

"Pray you came armed with more than brave words and iron-tipped sticks!" the dragon snarled, exposing row upon row of yellowed teeth.

Von Bompus tugged at his mustache with a casual air. "Beastie, I've the means to subject you to my will."

The dragon huffed, spilling green acid from the gaps between its teeth. "You're not the first to make that claim! Why, I do believe I've crushed some of your ancestors. Surely your King Santrop could have sent more than Sir Doddering Old Fool!"

The dragon laughed at his own joke.

"Damn you," von Bompus cursed. "You will surely bow before me, monster, at the utterance of your name!" The arch knight reached into his pouch and pulled out his dragon scale—the mystic catalyst for enslaving the beast—at least, thus spoke the holy books of Kinrae, the elvin deity who chained the beast to this forsaken place.

"My name? Many have claimed both my name and scale before," mused the dragon.

Von Bompus remained unflappable. "The king's own mage forced your name from a demon's mouth. I now bear it seared in my mind like a flaming brand. But enough! Angor Zap Koranikum Pantalengic—I command you to turn over your wealth to me, by the power of your own name!"

The dragon gasped. Vapors of steam leaked from its nostrils as if from a doused fire.

Von Bompus's cheeks flushed in delight. But the troopers behind him fidgeted nervously. Von Bompus cast a hand behind himself to quell their disquiet as long heartbeats passed without movement from the beast. Then it shuddered, a great terrifying trembling as if caught in the apoplexy, and gnashed its teeth. Clearly struggling deep within itself, it drew a frighteningly deep breath and lifted its head to the vaulted cavern ceiling.

The dragon braced its feet and blasted a great roar of fire toward the rim overhead. The troops, von Bompus included, fought hard to control their mounts as dripping tongues of flame coursed down the rock faces around them to sputter out on the floor.

Unseen in the shadows, Vondrall dropped the last few feet off the rope and prayed the beast didn't turn around.

When the flame was finally exhausted, the dragon drew breath again and let out another blast of anguish—three times in all—until the men's ears were ringing. It took all of Vondrall's control to retain his footing as he skittered in terror across the mounds of gold.

At last the dragon crumpled to the floor, gasping for air, its eyes wide and its mighty jaw slackened.

Turning in the saddle, von Bompus gestured for his troops to reform.

"How?" chugged the beast in a broken voice.

"Angor Zap Koranikum Pantalengic," the arch knight replied, using the name as he might an old friend's. "It only took a day for Cambric, the king's wizard, to discover the hell spawn charged with guarding it."

The dragon lifted its head; tears poured down its face in heated streams. "Sir Derring von Bompus," the dragon said, stretching a clawed forepaw and bowing low before the warrior. "You are truly the cleverest of all the humans to enter my home."

Von Bompus nodded regally in acknowledgment of the compliment.

Vondrall padded carefully around the back of the chamber, his eyes darting between his prize and von Bompus. He needed to claim the orb while the arch knight kept the beast occupied, for the name von Bompus had used *was not the one the elves had been given*. They would have stood no chance on their own.

"To you I pass not only my treasure, but also the secrets of my lair," the dragon continued, prostrating itself before the arch knight.

Von Bompus's face glistened, beads of sweat forming glorious jewels of victory across his brow. He spurred his mount forward.

"Now, dragon, as your master, I command you to yield up not just your wealth, but also the secrets of which you spoke."

"Yes, secrets," it hissed.

"I shall have them," demanded the arch knight.

"And you shall—you have the right," the dragon murmured, dragging itself to its feet once more. "Know this, human, the secrets I tell strike terror in the hearts of all who hear them. They will be the very last you remember on the day your body grows cold."

"Tell me!" commanded the arch knight, leaning closer to catch every word.

"Then listen, Derring von Bompus of Solorent," the dragon whispered. "For this is the secret of Dragon Home. Demons can be bought, and dragons lie!"

The startled look on von Bompus's face was cut short—for the dragon's teeth squashed his head, spattering gobbets of blood and brain across his saddle.

The enraged dragon thrashed its great tail, throwing the troopers into a wild panic. A screaming horse spattered against the nearby wall. Vondrall took advantage of the confusion to lunge for the orb, snatching it into the cradle of his arms to recklessly sprint back toward the rope.

But the dragon's tail swung again, shattering loose rock and snagging the lifeline out of the elf's reach. Vondrall rolled behind a large shield leaning against an outcropping, hoping the worst would pass him by. What few troopers survived fled from the cavern, with the dragon spitting liquid fire in their wake. Vondrall pressed against the shield as cries of pain flooded back into the lair.

"Truly, von Bompus will be remembered as a *fool of fools!*" the dragon crowed, then began scratching at the roasted flesh at its feet. "By my name, Yim Zamur op Shamalonai, I am the most powerful of all creatures!"

Shivers raced up and down the elf's spine—for that wasn't the name he'd been given either! His joints turned to jelly as he thought about how close he had come to ending up like von Bompus. He peered around the shield to watch the dragon settling into the carnage.

Far above, Gunolf leaned over the rim, pulling at the rope. But it remained impossibly out of reach. He signaled for Vondrall to remain hidden, then he disappeared. Moments later, another rope flopped to the ground, the end curling up about ten paces away. Vondrall glanced at the glutted dragon, seemingly falling once more into sleep, then scurried for the rope. The elf's shoulder clipped the edge of the shield, sending it spinning. *Clank, clank, clank!* The war board crashed into a pile of goblets, eventually wobbling to rest on a serving plate.

The dragon's head jerked up, its cold eyes immediately riveting on the elf. Vondrall heard a hiccupping, belching sound and dropped to the ground as searing liquid fire exploded all around him. Precious metals ignited and melted while sizzling gases erupted into the air. Vondrall staggered to his feet, struggling to blurt out the dragon's name.

"Watch out!"

The dragon's head jerked up and the beast screamed in rage.

Valerian perched on the rim, squawking like a mad crow. The dragon sucked in a breath, then blasted a stream of fire at him. Flames exploded across the rim, lighting up the cavern in sulfurous colors.

"No!" Vondrall cried, clenching his own piece of dragon scale in his hand. "You will stop, Yim Zamur op Shamalonai!"

The dragon kinked its neck around and roared with horrid mirth. It was then that Vondrall realized the scale would do him no good.

The dragon inhaled charred air for a final blast.

Vondrall murmured a few words in the elfin High Tongue, engaging the spell prepared in the nether. He vanished, but the dragon released its heated breath, yellowed flames washing over the space Vondrall had occupied moments before. Stone and metal ran together like warm butter.

When the vapors cleared, the beast pawed at the remains, eyes shifting back and forth, scanning for charred flesh. "I know you're here, elfling," the serpent hissed.

With a blue flash, Vondrall leaped out of the nether near von Bompus's corpse. He clawed for the piece of scale still clutched in the dead knight's hand, but the fingers were frozen in death. In frustration, Vondrall jammed a finger into the clenched fist, touching the scale's smooth, leathery surface.

The dragon's hulking body twisted around to face him, flames drooling from its jaws.

"So, we've a magicker among us," the beast snickered.

"Yim Zamur op Shamalonai!" Vondrall panted the words. "I command you to stop!"

"Do you really think he had one of my scales?" Fiery liquid sprayed across the carnage and swirled in fumy heat around the elf.

But Vondrall had already snatched another spell from the nether, the other dimension wrapping around his body and pulling him from certain death once again. In the grey half-light, the elf brushed at the glowing embers smoking on his breeches. And in that dim refuge, he determined there remained but one way to get a scale.

The beast was warily circling its lair when from high above a hoot caught its attention. It rose up on its haunches, craning for a better look, and found a grizzled elf with a silvery beard letting out another whoop, poking out his tongue, and waving his arms. Yim Zamur op Shamalonai belched heat from its gullet, splashing flaming death over the rim.

A blue light flashed and Vondrall rushed from the nether. He scurried beneath the dragon's exposed underside, frantically searching among the smooth, ordered scales. The dragon sucked air in for another blast when Vondrall found and tugged on one askew from the others. The beast's muscles rippled beneath, tossing the elf off his feet, but Vondrall hung on, twisting the scale until it tore free.

"Yim Zamur op Shamalonai, don't move! Just stop!"

Furiously the dragon shook and snarled, infernal rage stoppered up within its gullet.

Vondrall edged toward the rope, holding the heavy scale before him like a shield, the sack with the bauble slung over his shoulder. "I've got all I want! Now just let me go and this will be the last you see of us!"

The dragon slithered forward, its eyes a baleful red. Its snaking tongue licked across the floor, shoveling aside gleaming treasure and dark rubble. The dragon wagged a claw at Vondrall's face. "You've been lucky thus far."

Vondrall choked on the vapors. Repeating the dragon's name once more, he stepped determinedly toward the rope.

The ancient wyrm lifted its body to its full height, unfolding great black wings that beat against the sides of the cavern. "Leave!" he spat in great fiery bouts. "Leave before I forget the bounds put upon me by that damnable Kinrae!"

Vondrall straightened defiantly to full height before the beast. He was no longer Vondrall the Command Fourth—rather he was the only power standing between the beast and his men. When he spoke, each word echoed through the lair. "By the power of your name and the articles of your imprisonment, you will let us leave! And the terms shall be to the end of your days! Be satisfied that I've taken nothing else!"

"Enough!"

"No, not until the agreement is concluded! And once agreed, by the power of your name, then it will be enough. Then I'll go!"

The dragon's nostrils flared wickedly. Finally, the word hissed from its gullet. "Agreed."

Vondrall tied the rope around his waist, gave it a jerk, and his companions hauled him out of the dragon's lair.

"Come on, come on." Gunolf was fumbling desperately at the bindings when Vondrall reached the top. "Don't stand there gawkin' at me like I'm a ghost. If that dragon hadn't been so mad, I'd be crisper than a slab of bacon in my wife's kitchen."

Vondrall stumbled after his rangers into the depths of the rock—back along the dark, twisting track. The stone rumbled beneath their feet with the dragon's distant laughter. The elves hurried among the outcroppings and stumbled into wrong turns in their haste to return to the surface. Upon finally reaching the mountain's treacherous slope, they scrambled in the waning sunlight down the rope lines and footholds. But ever on their heels, the quaking continued until the clouds atop the mountain shredded into wispy tendrils. Fire and brimstone spouted into the air, and a great shadow erupted from the depths and into the night sky. The elves dove for cover among the nooks and crannies in the broken stone.

"Enough!" the maddened dragon screamed, circling the summit on great wings. "No one has stolen from me—ever!"

Valerian, nursing a burn on his cheek, grabbed at Vondrall's arm as he stepped from the shadows of their granite spar. "Stay. If you try to sweet-talk it, you'll get fried."

"If I don't, you all will." Vondrall clasped the veteran's arm in a sign of camaraderie. "Just be sure to get them all home."

Valerian nodded reluctantly, returning the grip on Vondrall's arm. "As you order, Command First," he said with a conviction that Vondrall could not spend time savoring. He stepped out into the open and held the single dragon scale above his head.

"The challenge has been met, and the contract is confirmed!" Vondrall shouted into the tornado whipping about him.

"Thief!" the beast shrieked. "You've stolen both my name and my riches!"

The dragon sucked in air like a great bellows, stoking the fires within to the brilliance of an overheated forge. It shot across the sky, the beast's innards glowing with an infernal fire.

"Then take me! But, before Kinrae, you're in breach of your own name's binding!"

The words had barely left the elf's lips when the heavens cracked with jagged lightning.

The dragon trumpeted defiance.

Atop Thunderer's mangled peak appeared a figure from within in a confluence of storm energy. The figure was taller than a frost giant, but was bearing the slender form of an elvin warrior. This angelic being was clad in armor that shone like a silvery moon. Upon his head sat a tall, conical helmet with a visor covering his face. Laughter echoed through the broken landscape as the warrior hefted an immense ax that in his skilled hands flowed through various defensive wards in a blur.

Earth and sky groaned when the dragon launched toward the warrior, beating the air on great veined wings. It shrieked at the newcomer who could only be Kinrae—the very god who had wrestled the wyrm into the pit and bound it by the power of its own name. Now here he stood once again, boots planted astride the summit, to enforce the terms of that imprisonment. The collision of the age-old combatants shattered spars of rock. Vondrall covered his face with his hands as he staggered back toward his comrades. Razored shards cut his skin as they rained down the slope. Flashes of gold swirled in the night sky to be beaten back by black, leathery wings. Then a brilliant rain scattered across the mountain. Or what Vondrall took to be rain.

For where the glowing drops soaked the parched earth, life sprang in abundance. Plants, green and leafy, exploded upward into the night. Some took root on bare stone, while others blossomed in crevices, their roots reaching into the mountain's hide, heaving and breaking the surface. Then the cloud of darkness blew down a black rain that blotted out the stars and cast a nightmarish pall over the slope. Where those dark drops touched the plants, twisted thorny brambles emerged. Dark and light runoff mixed in pools amid the crags, with life springing forth—but they were horrid creatures, twisted, with long serpents' bodies. Where the brilliant liquid pooled undisturbed, different creations emerged from the murk, these resembling the fairy cousins of the elves. Dark drops seared their skin, causing them to cry out and to seek shelter.

Amid the creation myth run amok, the elves focused on their own immediate needs. Twill smeared salve on burns and torn flesh, with Vondrall at his elbow tearing strips of bandages to be applied as directed. Valerian fought against the encroaching misshapen serpent spawn, his saber flashing against the storm-wracked sky. Gunolf led the others into creating makeshift defenses by weaving together the erupting branches.

From the darkness that surrounded them, different noises chattered from the shadows. Vondrall glanced up from his work, focusing his night vision to peer into the shadows, where slithering, sinuous shapes rippled. He tied off a bandage, then drew his saber when the first serpentine head emerged over their bramble bulwark, long fangs dripping venom. He stabbed at it, but the creature darted away. The elves scrambled to secure their weapons, but the creatures suddenly overwhelmed them in a writhing mass. Wicked teeth sank into exposed flesh. Valerian, swinging until the end, fell amid a pile of severed serpents' heads, his blade still dripping gore when it slipped from his fingers. Cool stone touched Vondrall's back, yet he continued stabbing and cutting as the rest of his men fell one by one around him. He twisted it loose to face more creatures slithering toward him over the fallen bodies of his rangers. He hacked and stabbed, then hacked again, pushing into an explosion of black fluids.

A voice hissed in his mind, *These are not mine, but of Kinrae's own blood. His alone bears the power of life. They're not bound by my name!*

Vondrall cried out when teeth punched through his boot and into his calf. He stomped down on a serpent's head, crushing it, and sliced the serpent in half. He staggered, his leg aflame with pain. Nearby, a slithering body wriggled into his pack.

The orb.

He grabbed the exposed tail and whipped the serpent away. But many more slithered forward to take its place. One turned and spit venom. Its head popped into the air when Vondrall's saber parted its flesh. Again, Vondrall plunged into the black bodies. Fangs tore his flesh as he thrust his hand into the pack. The orb's surface was smooth beneath his fingers. He cradled it in his hand and lifted it out, all the while fighting with his other hand. But his weapon grew increasingly heavy until it slipped from his fingers. Marshaling what strength remained, he heaved the bauble up over his head.

I will have it back, echoed through his head.

Serpents knotted about his legs as he stumbled from the meager shelter and into the storm. The children of the dragon sank their teeth deep and clung to him. Then, from the sky, something wet hit the orb's smooth surface and ran in illuminated scarlet down its surface before dripping to the ground. Light burst from within the globe. The serpents released their fangs, dropping from Vondrall's legs and recoiling back into the shadows.

"Born of Kinrae, but you're still the dragon's get!" Vondrall spat.

He stumbled numbly down the slope, the poison burning through his body and blurring his vision. He followed the sound of the burbling liquid as it flowed past—Kinrae's blood bearing the power of life. Then his feet went numb and refused to move; his arms sagged against his will. Vondrall vomited and fell to his knees. Blood flowed from his nostrils before he hit the ground. But broken stone did not tear his skin.

The ground was blanketed in a lush, green carpet, and he inhaled the fragrance of woodland flora with each gasp. He fought to move his legs for just a few more steps, but he failed. He pushed up onto his elbows then, and like the serpents about him, crawled. A flat-headed beast raised its head to his eye level, fangs gleaming with poison.

"If you want this, then take it!"

Vondrall pushed the bauble at the creature, but it shrank from the stabbing light.

"Gods damn you, take it!"

But Kinrae's blood fired the orb, blinding even the elf. Vondrall held a shaking hand before his eyes. Squinting past the light, he saw the moving fluid and, with the last of his waning strength, rolled into the stream as the bauble tumbled away in the flow. The stream thickly gushed around him, covering and washing him in its driven current. He sputtered and held his breath as he struggled to find the orb, which rolled along, glowing brilliantly. He was drowning, his lungs burning for air. And in his mind came the whispered word, *breathe*—and breathe he did.

Renewal surged through his dying limbs and mind as he let go of his instincts and allowed Kinrae's blood to flood into his lungs. His soul felt a measure of rapture—peace amid the violent chaos that stormed across the skies. And it was in that peace the god's blood offered the antidote to the venom. The healing brought realization. Upon the slopes of the old stone pile his comrades lay dead or dying—collateral damage to the battle above. And yet he now could offer them the same measure of aid. He opened his eyes and saw the orb nearby. He scooped it up. His other hand he thrust toward the stream's surface, fingers extended. But there was no god to pull him up. So he kicked with all his might and burst above the surface. He swam across the current to the edge and dragged himself into the now verdant greenery that expanded beyond the ribbon of god's blood. At the stream's edge, he emptied his canteen's last briny drops, then scooped it deep into the flow, watching the bubbles rise until it was full.

The skies above crackled with lightning, casting horrific images across the mountain's heights. Vondrall stoppered the canteen. All about him life continued to crawl and slither from the depths. Some creatures were twisted by dragon's vitriol—other forms rushed on awkward limbs to find shelter. Vondrall had no time to marvel at how he was now touched by a god's blood. He staggered back up the slope toward the lonely strand of rock where his comrades had made their last stand. The orb lit the way, causing newly created elvish Folk to shield their eyes and serpent spawn to slither into the shadows at his passing. And in his elation, a familiar voice hissed in his mind and caused his god-touched body to tremble.

Beware the night, Vondrall of Elvin Home. For now, I know your name. There can be no hiding! Watch the shadows—where neither moons nor stars illuminate. For in that darkness, the fallen spawn of Kinrae, my children, will find you.

He laughed at the warning and held the orb high.

From deep within his soul, energy burned, welling up within his breast, and he felt it rush through his arms into the Orb of Solomnai. Light exploded from its depths, stabbing into the night with a ferocity that scorched the unholy spawn of Kinrae's blood tainted by the bleeding of the dragon. Scaly bodies shrank back even as they burned and sought shelter amid the dense undergrowth that now carpeted Thunderer's flanks. The elvish creations, those who bore the features of the Kinrae, shrank back at first, covering their eyes. But after a moment, they lowered their hands and stretched out their arms to face the light with peaceful looks upon their previously confused faces. One would have thought they stood within a distant glade during a long summer's day, soaking in the golden warmth of the sun. But none of that mattered to Vondrall, focused as he was on the combatants who raged far above the earth.

"No," he shouted into the storm. "I am Command First of the Second Squad of the Milvin Eagles. Because of you, I'm neither who I was, nor who I will become! You don't know me!" And it was true, for he'd been touched by a god's blood—and he could feel that promise coursing through his veins. But he'd also been tainted with the dark scourge that fell amid the great battle. Even though the dragon was a part of him, he was not cowed in fear.

For the dragon, the gods—none of them mattered. For all that mattered was binding up his comrades' wounds and returning home to deliver a royal promise.

ANGEL OF DARKNESS

Born of the union, fire, and lust
enveloped in fairest of carnal flesh,
white porcelain smoothed; lips of ruby
killed my immortal soul,
yes, in a single drop of blood,
rolling down your finger—
ebony thorn, the one blemish mars
yet another bloom-petaled
nocturnal rose.
Oberon, watch the faint heart
lapse 'tween sanity and fear,
droughts of lively thunder
seared in burning flesh.

Joined in an affection unsevered
amid the siren call of night;
nebulous time plots to steal her
away from the feeble grasp of day.
Minions of seconds and hours
conspire to separate the youth,
in flesh and in blood.
Riding the storms of age
inevitable the stealthy march,
dukes of the earth and sky
envy her every step with another.

Revel each slipping moment,
seizing the pain
of loss never regained,
even by firm fingers
'pon the pulsing throat of slippery time.
Between the tick and pendulum swing, she remains—
long after sensations of flesh
fade away—where memory, the master,
her face alone can regain.

DANCING WITH DEMONS

I am bound
Upon a wheel of fire, that mine own tears
Do scald like molten lead.

William Shakespeare
King Lear, IV, 45

No light, no sliver of hope shown through the cracks in the door. No windows punctuated the room's walls. All remained dark—darker than he had ever known; yet he did not care.

Why should he?

There was nowhere to run.

He closed his eyes.

Recent memories rollicked back and forth in his head, waves that stirred up renewed humiliation. All the tricks and lies that led to terribly misguided actions were now awash over him. He now wore the bounty of those actions as titles: betrayer of mankind, demon friend, destroyer of Annara, and slayer of the human race. Now, even the faintest touch of sleep brought back thousands of screaming accusations, wailing voices crying to the deaf ears of the heavens for vengeance. And, once the treacherous floodgates were let loose, there would be no stemming the torrent.

Eyes wet, he waited on the pleasure of his allies.

Hours, weeks, possibly months had passed since the beginning of his incarceration, when metal twisted in the lock, drawing the man's attention to the door. He stirred in the dirty straw as the portal screamed open on rusty hinges. A flickering torch was thrust into the room and a raspy voice called his name.

"Come, Morrin king. It's time." A bug-eyed creature poked its face through the doorway, mouth pulled back into a smile of pointy yellow teeth and stringy saliva. "Come. Come, you've been summoned to court." The creature cackled, waving to its companions beyond the door. There were murmurs in the corridor and four more faces peered inside.

Morrin, the last king of Annara, lifted his cramped body from the musty corner. Filthy bodies pressed against the prisoner and rough, scaly hands thrust him down the damp corridors. The foul breath falling hotly on Morrin's neck forced him to cough, and his eyes watered from the torches' oily fumes, yet the king, long used to being shut up, closed his mind to this reality and shut himself within the stolid bars of his own creation.

It had been some time since Morrin tried invoking magic that would empower him to escape. His hands twitched at the thought of the sorcerous might they once wielded, at the thought of his weapon. No, he wouldn't try to recall it, for it had caused many of his woes. Created by of a long-dead smithy who had captured a godling to acquire the requisite liquid for the tempering, Demonbane was the legendary sword that sang in battle. Once, by means of the hellish blade, the olden kings had protected humanity from the foul depredations of the demonic earth spawn. More recently, the last king had used it to lay waste to the entire human race. Morrin himself had been death's reaper, riding van to the victorious demonic forces after the storming of Vontan Diliak, the capital of Annara, and his birthplace.

Morrin, rightful king of Annara, lifted the battered helmet's visor so that he could better survey the gaping breach in the wall. The few remaining survivors in the citadel rushed to fill the hole, but the hordes of Shalzere already mounted the crumbled fortifications to sweep the faltering resistance aside. The king chuckled with ghastly delight, mimicking the sound emitted by the blade he swung over his head. He signaled the final charge. Atop his black stallion, the triumphant king of Annara rode through the melee, the great steel vampire in his hands cleaving through all, regardless of badge or livery, all the while singing a horrible song of death. The conflict stirred Morrin's blood, causing his eyes to burn. His temples throbbed with a sinister lust. He was lost in the blade, lost in the heat of battle, and lost in the hunger.

Only he who waited in the throne room could slake his dark thirst.

The tall steed waded through the sea of corpses filling the ruined courtyard, the despoiled remains of Annara's capital.

The walls of the citadel stood above the city, high atop Mont Kieraugh, defying the king to come farther, but Morrin knew the palace defenses to be but a small breaker wall of last resort, unable to keep the crashing sea of demons from finally overwhelming the remnants of Annara. Only a handful of royal guards bent their bows in defiance of the odds. The Shalzerian earth spawn shambled forward into the arrows and piled on top of each other, both the quick and the dead, forming a ladder of flesh to the battlements. The gates were quickly flung open and Morrin galloped through.

Oblivious to the slaughter around him, people the king had known since birth, Morrin rode across the courtyards and to the great doors of the palace proper. Within these once resplendent walls, the cycle of his journey would be completed.

The slavering demon hordes, chained beasts drooling for the holed-up fox, stood waiting.

The gold-leafed gates swung open. Morrin slapped his blade into its scabbard and spurred his mount forward to accept the invitation. The clatter of shod hooves rang off the rose-marbled floors. It was a noise absorbed in the vastness of columns, polished brass doors, and rich tapestries. The king knowingly threaded his mount at a trot through the opulent maze, his anger rising from deep within his chest as he approached the throne room.

"Enter my brother," the voice said as the door opened. Morrin slid from his mount and entered. At the far end of the chamber sat Roaric, the Usurper and self-proclaimed monarch of the realm. His hand rubbed at the rough stubble on his chin and his face was drawn and gaunt beneath the heavy rosy-gold crown of Annara.

"I do believe you've come for this, what little good it will do you." Roaric smiled, tapping his temple just below where the crown pressed his flesh.

"Yes, I've come for both," Morrin sneered. "I trust the siege hasn't inconvenienced you, brother." A half-brother of dubious claim to the name and the distant Freacht March, let alone the throne of the realm.

"Oh, come now." Roaric leaned forward and spat. "You've no time to worry about me when you and your comrades have celebrating to do. You are celebrating this victory, aren't you?"

Morrin smiled. "Yes, I suppose I will celebrate your death."

Roaric shook his head, narrowing his eyes at his brother. "Do you hate me so much that it was worth laying waste the entire kingdom?"

"Yes." Family, hearth, and home—it was all gone. Roaric had taken it with the support of a powerful court faction.

"Then, let it finish here." Roaric stood, his tall frame encased in silver embossed plate. He hefted a two-handed landsknecht sword from beside the throne, and the serpent-twisted blade shimmered, giving it the appearance of living steel.

"Yes, it shall end here," Morrin agreed as he scraped Demonbane free from its scabbard. With his free hand, he began hurling previously prepared magicks at his brother's own sorcerous defenses...

"You shall run in madness, like kings of olden days," bubbled through Roaric's frothing lips when he died a broken wreck there at the foot of the throne.

Stern hands steadied Morrin, keeping the king trudging forward among the dancing shadows. The corridor snaggled deep into the earth's bowels, snaking closer and closer to the throne room of the demon lords. Gritting his teeth, Morrin kept shuffling ahead, plodding one foot ahead of the other. Eventually, torchlight dazzled his eyes and, with his vision clearing, the king focused on the picture of the immense chamber. Beyond the howling hordes of the underworld that filled the chamber sat the enthroned Lords of Shalzere—the masters of the lower realm and, of late, conquerors of the upper. These were Morrin's allies and sworn friends.

Those many days, weeks, or months ago, black cloak swirling about his scarlet buckskin boots, the young king first swept into the chamber, enwrapped in a confident air. The demon courtiers eyed him with suspicion, though none dared raise a weapon against him, for it was rumored the human bore the legendary blade of kings, the Demonbane. Morrin laughed at their timidness, mockingly clucking his tongue when they retreated out of reach.

Beware, the king thought, *lest I split your skulls.*

Morrin began weaving a spell of protection as he mounted the lower steps of the dais. These, these were the makings of a wicked army, an army that would bring Roaric down. Yes, a good strong magick was in order. On this occasion, minor demons hissed and spat like sizzling bacon grease, parting right and left to let Morrin pass through their midst. Foul spittle huffed through the air, coating Morrin's exposed flesh in sticky mucus. The king avoided looking into the mob's faces, his watering eyes drawn to the dais at the head of the hall where the three demon lords waited: Almuc of the Fist, Merazio the Slayer, and Serampin of the Long Darks, the earthspawn Triumvirate.

Never in his wildest dreams had Morrin imagined their aid would bring about not only his brother's death, but also the wholesale destruction of his realm. Nor had Morrin realized how eager Demonbane would be to draw blood—rich, red human blood—until the foul deeds were already done.

They forced the king to his knees at the rugged, basaltic steps of the dais. Morrin looked up and saw the great black blade clenched in the skeletal hands of the hooded Serampin, the only sorcerer besides himself capable of containing the weapon. The blade sighed, but the burning desire to wield it no longer heated Morrin's soul; the blood of his enemies no longer wetted his lust for revenge.

Almuc raised his voice across the chatter-filled hall, the demon's pig-like face smiling. "King Morrin, we hope your chambers of state have been adequate." Almuc's red eyes gleamed with mirth, his gargantuan body jostling with laughing snorts. "We know you must be about the myriad of duties befitting one of your rank."

Laughter rose to ear-piercing levels.

Morrin didn't respond. He knew the outcome of this final audience and had accepted that death would soon entangle his wyrd. There was no reason to expend energy on petty barbs cast at his conscience. He wanted death, though Morrin wondered if hell could be worse than imprisonment in subterranean Shalzere.

Demonbane moaned.

Merazio raised a large, horny hand and silence fell across the chamber. The creature's scale armor clanked and grated as Merazio lifted his heavy, bone-crushing mace over his head. The king knew Merazio well. Only recently they had fought side by side in the gory streets of Candhera and Vontan Diliak as comrades in arms. Merazio the Slayer was well versed in the exquisite music of death.

The demon's voiced thundered aloud.

"Brethren, from the beginning of time, when our first fathers crawled from the primeval ocean slime to the dry earth, we have been subjected to the humors of man. This time is past!"

The demonic hordes of Shalzere erupted in approval. Merazio again raised his hand for silence.

"For four thousand long years we have been forced to dwell in the deepest pits. This exile in darkness has also ended! Precious man has been wiped from the face of the world!"

Merazio lowered the mace. A group of demons surged forward, a large wooden box on their horned shoulders. They upended it at the base of the throne, depositing the contents in a grisly scatter across the floor—dismembered human flesh.

Morrin thought it a fitting visual for a victory oration.

"Now the victors will set in motion a new age, an age in which Shalzere shall rule the surface. An age devoid of man!" Merazio's red-eyed gaze fell on Morrin. "The weapon holding the balance of power in man's favor these centuries must be destroyed," Merazio continued, "followed by the demise of the last king."

Almuc snorted.

Morrin was pulled to his feet by vile hands that indiscriminately tore his clothes and flesh. The last king of man was hauled from the pits of the underworld. He looked forward to his impending death, his escape.

Crowding demons rimmed the sulfurous mouth of Ciarna Ectam Na. Molten rock spewed red bubbles from the volcano's cracks, seeping down its sides like slow weltering tears. The sky churned above as dark clouds swirled, enveloping the natural blue.

Demon wizardry clawed Ciarna's summit with bitter, biting winds.

Morrin's captors held him firmly near the bubbling pit, and through watery eyes he saw the shrouded Serampin emerge like a flitting wraith on the opposite side of the steamy maw. Serampin, whose powers rivaled those of Morrin's own family, held the mystic sword Demonbane, its runes squirming helplessly up and down the blade's black steel. The jewels in the skulled hilt gleamed and sparkled like clots of fresh blood. The sword cooed to Morrin, but the king didn't listen.

Serampin raised Demonbane above his head, then the demon lord sang. The song was centuries old when the world was new; a song whose words of magic flowed like a searing iron through the stricken air. Power rushed into Ciarna's gurgling lava and began constructing a magical pattern, the matrix of undoing.

A wan smile twisted Morrin's thin lips. He realized that only warm, sticky human blood could complete the spell, his blood, releasing the magic trapped within the steel. Through Morrin's veins pulsed the last remaining drops of the now precious stuff. Thus, Roaric's death curse would not come to fruition.

The demon lord cast the sword into the molten pit, the blade straight as if it had stuck in the jugular of the very earth itself. Heat crawled up the length of the black steel, the runes writhing in fiery crimson. The sword let loose a piercing cry, sending chills up the king's back, but Morrin fought to shut it out though his heart pounded to respond.

By all the gods and the sins on my shoulders, let it finish. "End it," he muttered.

On the far side of the inferno, demons carried out a tattered sack, dumping it on the ground. Serampin loosed the cords on top and reached in. Effortlessly the demon pulled out a twisted, skinny wrist, followed by the rest of a kicking, screaming man. The sobbing wretch was forced to his knees at the demon lord's feet.

Morrin's head drooped, his chin quivering slightly. He was much too tired for the fresh infusion of emotions. Yes, much too tired. Lifting his eyes, the king grated his teeth. Of himself, he cared little, but he was no longer the last man as he had been led to believe. By all the gods of hell, he wished to let the drama run the course of the last act.

"No," he groaned. Sweat dripped down his forehead, running down his flushed cheeks like streams of lava. Morrin wrestled with sensations he'd not felt since before his exile from Annara. The king clenched both hands into white-knuckled fists.

This was my death—this was to be mine.

Demonbane howled, harmony to the final chord.

Knowing full well the heavy toll the blade would exact on the creatures around him, Morrin called out in the high language of Annara's sorcerer kings, the words touching his cracked lips in a soothing caress. "Come to me. Demonbane, come." A hand clapped over his mouth, but it could not stifle the call borne from the heart, a heart bound to the vampire magicks of the blade.

A hellish shriek of jubilation trilled as the sword sprang from the molten rock in a flurry of spattering lava. Serampin's spell was broken. Glowing cherry red, the sword winged through the grey light. Demons skittered to and fro, releasing the captive king in the confusion. Morrin felt his fingers clamp down on the hilt; a scream wrenched from his throat as the blade's magic encircled his hands. They had become one again.

Demonbane yowled unholy delight, its beastly hunger loosed.

The last king of Annara swept through the close-pressed crowd, searing a path of death into the floundering hordes of Shalzere and driving the creatures back to their underworld home. Morrin lost himself in the familiar berserk lust, and he relished it.

Almuc's cat and mouse game had gone awry, yet Serampin retained his cool composure as Morrin fought closer and closer along the volcanic ridge. Prudent wisdom had not been enough to prevail against the bullish demon lord's desire to degrade Morrin one final time, and now the wily Serampin was left alone to stave off the mad king's rage.

The demon lord faced the king, his black cloak snapping in the wind. He raised a crooked finger, hurling a crackling bolt of energy toward Morrin. The king barely turned the force off Demonbane's blade, sending up a brilliant halo of sparkles. The impact threw him into a pile of debris at the crater's edge. Morrin struggled to his feet and, rallying his strength, launched himself at Serampin. Demonbane sang gleefully as it sliced apart the few creatures brave enough to protect their master. Bursting past the corpses, Morrin plunged the blade to the hilt into the black figure.

The cowl shredded, Demonbane howling as it hungrily bit air.

Serampin had escaped to the deepest pit in the Shalzerian court.

Morrin raged a fist at the sky, cursing with vile words he'd learned during his forced sojourn in the world. His long blond hair blew in tangled strands, his eyes flashing with a consuming madness. He looked down at the trembling heap that lay on the ruined earth near the demon lord's smoldering cloak. The man looked up, his eyes meeting Morrin's own burning orbs.

"Wh— Who are you to take up the king's own sword?" he asked, squirming in the black dirt. Saliva dribbled out of his toothless mouth and down his stubbly chin.

"I am the king." Morrin's eyes cleared. He shook the bloodlust from his mind. "I am the king of Annara."

"You? You are King Morrin? Why—you betrayed us!" The man's eyes darted back and forth.

Morrin bent down near the man.

Absolution.

This was his chance to explain to another human, to be forgiven of all the terrible things.

"Listen," he whispered desperately.

"No!" the man shrieked. "No! I'll have nothing to do with you."

"You don't understand. I didn't mean to..." Morrin pleaded, heart pounding in his throat. "Listen!"

"No, I won't!" The man teetered to his wobbly feet. "Go tell your own ghosts!" He shrugged free of Morrin's grasp and darted for Ciarna's crumbling edge. The lava eagerly bubbled, steam hissing into the air.

"Stop!"

The man scrambled across the shattered rocks, and for the slightest moment he hesitated on the crumbling brink of the fiery pit. A blast shot up its glowing sulfurous discharge, singeing the man's hair. He cackled as Morrin reached for him, but too late; the man plunged into the volcano's steamy womb.

"No!" Morrin choked, his fingers clawing desperately at the ground, nothing but rocks falling through his fingers. The king collapsed, looking down at the glowing liquid swirling around, and around, and around. The infernal heat melted flesh off the man's bones, leaving only his gruesome face grinning eternally in Morrin's mind as it burst into flames. The last man, who was once a king, lay still for a moment before he slid away from the precipice.

Demonbane lay propped against a rock, sighing softly, its ghoulish appetite having been glutted for the time being. Morrin turned his head from the blade, the very sight of its gore-spattered surface disgusting him. The king laughed, tears running down his cheeks and dripping off his dirty chin to the sooty earth. The more he cried, the harder he laughed a maddening sort of mirth overcame him and, with his hands savagely clawing the air, he ran recklessly down Ciarna Ectam Na, chasing demons who were no longer there.

SPLENDOR

The bloody marred blade lays

nak'd upon a rock.

The knight, armor battered, fallen

not far off.

His hands outstretched, still

in death he grasps

for that familiar hilt.

Warrior's noble horse

calls up on the hill.

There is no one to answer,

no one who ever will.

With hands outstretched, still

in death they grasp—

the descending cloud

of crows.

FROM BEYOND THE GRAVE

Dead. The report indicated that the sealed coffin was en route to Cleveland from New York on an evening flight. Craig put the papers down on his cluttered desk and, as if someone abruptly cut the strings holding up his wooden limbs, he collapsed onto his padded chair.

Dead. The word seemed so strange. So blunt—so dead—dead—dead.

He looked out the window, past one of the few remaining pictures of her. Streams of water ran down the windowpane, wrinkling the grey autumn day beyond. A bird flitted past, seeking the dry shelter of its nest tucked up under the eaves. Children laughed through the puddles in the neighbor's backyard, spattered with green and brown, smiles of gap-toothed white.

But, inside this house, Death, that mysterious specter, enshrouded Craig's mind with thoughts of distant past. Time melted away with recollections of a previous spring full blooming in the small college town. Trees, leaves, and flowers emerged from their winter hibernation to the warming sun's rays. With the welcome relief from ice and snow came the anticipation of the term's end. Yet it was no time to be hidden away in the murky shadows of a classroom or stuffy corners of an office piled to the ceiling in yellowing books.

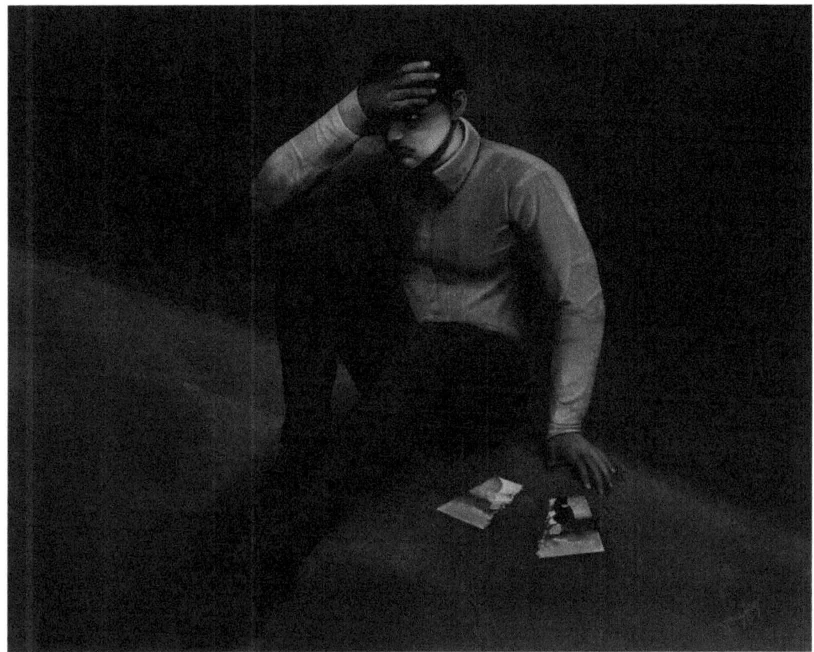

The young professor's step fell a little quicker and a carefree smile replaced the usual thoughtful reflections that lined his face. On one of these bright days, Craig found the acceptance letter for his manuscript in his office mail, along with one of many phone messages from his wife. She would be home late from her class. It all happened at the same time. Yes, it must have been the late nights, the manuscript—it all must have happened about the same time.

He thumped his fingers on the edge of the desk. There had been no time for one more dance in the bone-white gazebo at the center of the town square.

She arrived home late every night for a week, yet he thought nothing of it. Had he not acquired that habit with his own late nights through graduate school? Yes, he had and he clearly remembered why.

"So," Professor Montcalm mumbled, as he smoothed the edges of his bushy brown mustache. "You want to pursue a doctorate? You want to become an intellectual?"

Craig nodded uneasily. The wizened scholar halted his words for a moment and rifled through a pile of papers that lay atop his cluttered desk. Then, as if channeling Delphic inspiration from the divine, the patriarchal man scrunched up his nose and latched his focus back to the young wanderer, the traveler about to step on the hallowed path that few dared. A smile parted Montcalm's lips.

"You must be prepared at the outset to take to your bedside a mistress, one who will comfort you during the long, lonely nights: knowledge. She must consume you as hotly as the most passionate lover. Knowledge will become your intimate—the endpoint of her your consuming quest."

Of course, Montcalm's own marriage had been fully drained by the life-stealing succubus he fawned after during that journey. Craig paid a sufficient price and understood Diane's late nights, or so he thought. Alone in their large old home, snuggled deep in the sleepy college town, he rewrote his manuscript and tinkered about the house. When she'd arrive home from long days of study and work, he good-naturedly displayed the new faucets, the fresh paint, a polished chapter, or the dinner waiting cold in the refrigerator. At times she responded pleasantly, but more often she did not. Arguments erupted over a torn newspaper, the fat content in a gallon of milk, and who turned off the television, driving a sharp stake into the young marriage's heart.

Craig watched helplessly as the anchor mooring his life cranked up and the secure vision of hearth and home was sucked out into the retreating tide.

Diane came home later and later, always irritable.

"What have we gotten back for all those years of school, for your decision to study history of all things?" His profession more and more became the target for her sharpest barbs. "A job where we just make ends meet? I don't want to be a pauper the rest of my life. I've worked. I'm tired. I deserve more."

Craig reminded her that his first book's publication would certainly improve his status at the university. Regardless, she demanded to continue her advanced degree in a more lucrative field. Craig consented, managing to control the disappointment. He had looked forward to spending more time with his wife, but now it was her turn.

Did I really know her? he wondered, leaning back in his chair and staring up at the ceiling?

And now, she is dead.

He shook off the memories and the cobwebs to scan the report again. The police investigator filing the initial paperwork noted her whereabouts in New York and the man who had become her lover, a medical doctor specializing in some sort of long-winded procedure. She had run off, and now she returned in a box.

Why?

Why had her remains been sent back instead of being interred by her lover? Ironic, Craig mused sullenly, her lover could steal her soul but Craig ended up with her body. And he had never wanted just her body. His eyes darted around the room, blinking out a tear.

The police report stated that she ran out of the apartment complex where she lived and was struck by an oncoming car. Maybe they had argued. Maybe she had intended to return home.

Yes, she did come home, three and a half weeks later. Her body, sheathed in a sealed metal coffin, would be laid to rest in the young couple's plot in the local cemetery. A tall maple tree shaded the square of hillside overlooking a shallow ravine and slow-moving creek. There had been something eternal about the place, a sense of unchanging continuity between that plot and the quiet woods beyond town. At least that is what they talked about at the time.

Craig took out a pen and tapped it on the recently delivered insurance check. Good service.

He signed the back, intending to deposit it before going on to the red brick church where a small memorial was scheduled.

The panes of stained glass in the chapel looked menacing, the colored chips inky with only the grey rainy day outside to illuminate them. Lead-outlined images of the saints and the mother of God scowled like sinister specters, hiding in the vaulted shadows of the arches and windows. Craig sat sullenly on a chapel pew, wanting to focus on the minister's words, wanting to envelope himself in spiritual comfort, or even righteous indignation. He even tried hating Diane, but that emotion would take no permanent root in his heart. Wiping the tears from his face, he wondered what she thought of him before the vehicle struck. Or had she been so consumed by another?

He sat up and looked around the sparsely filled seats. Someone stood and left the back of the church, but, turning quickly at the noise, Craig did not see who it was. The minister finished his words, and Craig stood in the company of five men he knew from the university. Together, they hefted the coffin and solemnly strode out the side doors to the waiting hearse parked in the sprinkling rain. There would be no procession, no grand parade of death to the cemetery. The groundskeeper did not think the wet earth stable enough to use the heavy equipment necessary to bury her, at least not today.

Craig shook the hands of well-wishers and beat a hasty retreat to his car. He turned the key, started the vehicle, and pulled out behind the hearse. As he turned onto the town square, the bleached white frame caught his attention. Craig pulled into a parking place and got out of the car. He trotted across the sodden grass and climbed the wooden steps that led up to the platform of the gazebo. The rickety wooden structure stood amidst a ring of leafy maples, beneath the long shadow of the ivy-covered clock perched atop the courthouse tower. The clock struck two, loud reverberating booms that rattled the gazebo's loose floorboards. Craig's heart pounded as if to the faint echo of a distant drum, a drum throbbing to the beat of their favorite song. He caught his breath and placed one foot then another across the floor to the center, beneath the old cross beams to where they had once danced.

The memories seemed to take place in another lifetime, in another reality. It had been a warm night in August, the sticky air clinging to their clothes and limbs after the long drive. The rented moving van's seats shone in the fading sun, slick and uncomfortable. They ached to stretch their legs.

The gazebo came into sight as they approached the stoplight—the marbled remains of the wooden Parthenon caught in the yellowed glare of the streetlight and flickering fireflies. Craig stopped the truck and pulled Diane by the hand in his wake. In his memories, the place burst with an enchanted air, sparkling with a peaceful magic.

"My dear, may I?" he whispered in her ear as they began moving to a subtle rhythm in that mystical, midwestern Stonehenge.

Craig scraped his fingernail into the powdering cracks and curling peels of paint along the damp rail. Time had repainted the picture. His eyes swept across the platform to the blackened bones of a burnt-out house across the street to the east, then back to the antique shops and closed-up corner drugstore to the west. He glanced at his watch; the town clock was slow and he had to get to class. Yet for a brief moment her faded cotton shirt pressed on his arm, and the scent of her hair caused his heart to stir to the beat of a silent band.

Later that evening, Craig paced up and down his study, the only room of the house that insulated him from her. He stopped in front of the window. Rain continued falling. They couldn't backfill the grave until the rain stopped. The cemetery custodian didn't want to uncover the rest of the dead in the process of covering over this one.

In the faint glow of the back-porch light, a figure moved across the yard, stopping momentarily near the swing strung from the oak tree. Craig squinted, then darted for the door. He skidded across the porch, down some steps, and into the wet grass. Before he could catch his breath, the figure was gone. A shiver ran down his spine; he'd read too many Stephen King novels. There was no terrifying creature, created from his wife's decaying remains, lurking about in wait to rip off his head—just the soft patter of rain rustling the leaves in the tree and the echoing repeat of a neighbor's barking dog.

Baffled by his own stupidity, Craig returned to the house.

The next morning, he drove by the cemetery on his way to work. The plastic draped coffin lay on a sling over the plot, flowers bunched around with their sodden petals drooping in the rain, colors running out of the ribbons and into the mud.

Craig slogged up to the coffin and touched the tarp.

"Are you in there, Diane?" he whispered. "I want you to know—I still love you. Please forgive..." He couldn't think of the conclusion to his statement.

Of course he'd not been the perfect husband. How many times had he left her, regardless of her fervent pleas for him to stay? How often had he returned home from impassioned liaisons with his studies and been less than pleasant with her? Intellectual stimulation could burn in his chest the way she could. Their heat had been true passion, and it would never be rekindled.

Craig pulled the thin gold wedding band from his finger and laid it under the plastic against the cold coffin.

At the end of a long day, Craig trudged up the creaky old steps to his study. He sank into his chair, rested his arm on the smudged, doodle-covered blotter, and drummed his fingers against the desk.

Maybe I should sell the house, he thought. *I've really no use for something this large.* The phone rang. He tried to ignore its trill chatter, preferring the dynamics of his own thoughts. It rang again, and again, and again. Finally, Craig reached for it.

"Hullo," he said.

"Is the wife there?" a muffled male voice asked.

A chill shivered Craig to the spine. "She's not here."

The call cut off with a short click, and then the dial tone wailed. He looked at the number on the caller ID, but it was blocked like most telemarketers. Craig hung up the phone and leaned back in the chair until his head lolled against the warm radiator under the window. He looked up at the top of the windowpane, rolling the voice over again in his mind.

She's not there? Slowly he sat up, running his fingers through his hair, his eyes darting back and forth from his messy desktop to Diane's picture. No, that would be too bizarre. People just don't make phone calls like that. The phone remained silent, and he answered his imagination by going to bed.

The third full day after Diane's memorial, the rain stopped. The clouds thinned to blue, and fragmented sunshine penetrated to the earth as Craig walked back from the university library to his office above the History department. An official-looking form of some sort for the burial was tucked into his mailbox. Without reading it, he pressed the tip of a pen through the carbon copies, refolded it, and creased it neatly into the self-addressed, stamped envelope. He dropped it into the department's outgoing mail and went home.

Craig brushed his teeth, sloshing the foam around in his mouth. He looked at himself in the mirror and winced. The face staring back was drawn, black shadows clinging to his eyelids and red flecks spotting the whites of his eyes. Maybe he'd rest better tomorrow after Diane's coffin was covered over with dark Ohio earth. He shook his head and wandered off to bed.

The phone rang, and rang, and rang. Craig jolted up off the pillow. He grabbed the receiver. "Yes?"

"Are you sure your wife's not there? Are you sure of where she is?"

Craig perked up, shaking the cobwebs of sleep from his brain.

"Waddya mean where she is?" he asked angrily. "She's dead. What are ya calling me at..." He looked at his alarm clock. "It's two thirty in the morning."

"If you don't look for yourself, tomorrow will be too late."

Craig opened his mouth to say something, but the caller clicked the phone off. Tomorrow? The only thing going on tomorrow was a simple matter of landscaping—her final farewell.

The moon cast a silvery light over the edge of town where the cemetery lay behind tall iron fences. In that section of land rested the earliest settlers of the town, even those who had crossed bayonets with the British during the war of 1812. Five generations of Craig's family lived and died in this small town. He slowly pulled up to a side street and let the car coast to a halt. He turned off the car engine and felt a pang in his chest when he gazed into the rows of shadowed tombstones. The entrance was locked for the night behind tall, wrought iron gates. He quietly closed his car door, pulled the collar of his coat up, and slowly walked down the street to where the fence took a sharp ninety-degree turn and skirted into a shadowy wood. He found a foothold in the depths then hopped the wrought iron fence and scampered through the tombstones, across the sloshy grass to Diane's open grave.

The casket lay in the sling, cradled over the cool, recently cut-open earth, a darkened maw that threatened the flowers arranged in a pile near the end of the grave. Craig stepped slowly up to the casket, pulling the key from his pocket. He peeled back the plastic cover. The gruesome thought of opening the casket had never crossed his mind; the reports clearly stated that the car mutilated her. In fact, the container probably hadn't been opened since an examiner sealed it in New York. The key sprung easily in the lock with a click. He bent his back and pushed against the lid.

Craig stopped. A sick feeling twisted in his gut at the thought of looking at the mangled, decaying face of the woman he loved, the woman who betrayed him. Sucking a breath of air between his clenched teeth, he gave the last push and opened the casket.

Empty.

The interior was pristine crushed velvet, frilly lace, a smooth silken pillow.

Craig's legs wobbled as he leaned over the grave.

No body.

Footsteps sucked in the mud. Craig turned around and faced her. She stood silhouetted in the pale moonlight, jacket pulled up close about her neck. Craig looked back at the empty container, then at her. She smiled and took a step forward.

"You didn't really think I was dead, did you?" Her lips were wet with the mist from her breath.

"But you left." Craig shook his head, not believing; a bitter bite of bile stung the back of his throat. Why did she come back? She was dead. His mind spoke faster than his mouth. He took a tentative step forward; his hand reached as if to touch her cheek.

Her smile twisted and her eyes flashed. Craig thought he heard, "Didn't you leave me all those years?" as someone hit him over the head.

They were arguing about something, something about who would withdraw the money.

Money? What money? Craig's head throbbed behind his ear, his vision fuzzy and blurred. She said something about it being his fault. Whose fault? His fault? Malpractice? Craig was a doctor of philosophy, not a med...

They settled the argument with a few more clipped words, then silence.

Diane leaned over the open casket where Craig lay, expelling her sweet breath near his mouth. He imagined tasting her lips. He tried to move, but his body wouldn't respond. She smiled and said softly, "Damn malpractice. We can use the money."

"Can we get out of here? This place gives me the creeps," the other voice, a man's voice said. "In the morning, I'll take his signature to the bank and you get the tickets."

She kissed her finger and placed it on Craig's lip. The man pushed Diane out of the way. Craig saw the lid come down and heard the latch snap shut. The container jerked, then dropped when the sling was released. Craig groaned when it hit bottom.

Later, the air thickening in his burning lungs, Craig knew he hated her.

SIEGE

Crashing steel
Crumble the thunder
   as battle rolls down the shore.
Spattering, first a drop
opens to a torrent
of rain fell from above.
She'd called forth the elements
to soak us from the field.
Foul witch and sorceress,
keeper of magicks arcane,
I'd send you to hell for killing her
on this our wedding day.
Did you think to fill the void
now that love's grown cold?
Fie on the foul bats of your true love
brings to lay bloody at your step.
No, where sweet Elaine hath journeyed,
you'll not go; rather you
shall ride skewered atop a pike
about the castle walls.

Seat of thine kingdom, throne set in pearl,
all set in designs of murther.
Demons abound in your legions now,
have you been deserted by the living?
The castle looms large on the cliff,
overlooking Neptune's home,
her towers
a peaked thrust from hell,
set in the crags of Dragon Sound's Doom.
Still from the distance the
engines seek. Roar, roar your fury
'pon thatched roofs and
ancient walls.
For I shall have her
own foul blood
upon the ancient stone
of sweet Elaine's tomb.
The boom of the cannon
pounds with my heart, black
the kettle hurls stone.
Clouds of sulfurs stench billow
whispering the end of days.
Black bones shatter,
buttresses crumble with a pitch
and a roar as we charge the breach.

STARDUSTED

The *Lancelot II* thrust her mighty prow in a great surge into the heliosphere that represented the fringe of the solar system, muted gases parting around the vessel and leaving a wake behind in a lingering trail. The blue-grey alloy hull shimmered from the starlight brilliance of the plasma drive motor at the rear. Yet the smooth surface masked the deeper armor plating and shielding systems that braced the immense structure against the forces that would strain the ship during the test jump. Speeding around

Jupiter, Titan-based monitoring stations kept constant track of the behemoth craft as it cut into the vast void of open space. Its shape appeared to shorten as it approached the speed of light and prepared to jump beyond.

"Captain, the jump engines are ready. All systems check and go," said Lieutenant Rodriguez.

Derric adjusted the vector controls and nodded in agreement. "All hands prepare to enter pressure pods."

In a few minutes, the *Lancelot* would make the jump across the light barrier and the grav units would kick off, so everything would need to be buttoned down or risk becoming a projectile through the interior compartments. Butterflies tumbled around the captain's stomach. Simulations, no matter how detailed, could never predict what happened when a complex system went online. And this, the first test run of the plasma drive and the hyperjump past light speed was no different. Regardless, he kept reminding himself "just like the simulator."

Derric punched the intercom button to the engine room. "Status check."

"Had a bit of a problem, sir," Chief Rantson's voice calmly answered. "The nitro cooling pump exceeded tolerances and nearly burst a seal. But it's under control and all systems are nominal."

Derric tapped his finger on the control panel for a moment. A burst seal would put them back at Titan for another round of tests, simulations, and analysis. "Good. Keep an eye on the safety margin for me Rat. This has to go off without a hitch or we'll have bureaucrats up our ass."

"We're on it," Rantson replied. There was a hint of relief in his voice at the assurance the captain wasn't running back to Titan even now to spend another six months with engineers and safety inspectors tearing down and rebuilding systems for simulation analysis. Half the crew's hitch with the Space Agency would expire with another round, forcing the whole program into suspended animation while waiting for a rotation and another qualified crew.

"Lieutenant, check the trajectory along the run path."

"Onboard systems confirm control's scan. Avenue clear of debris."

"All right, everybody, into the pods."

The cabin crew automatically left their workstations and systematically filed into the pressure pods that lined the bulkhead. Every time Derric got in one, he thought of the man being buried alive in a casket. He chided himself for reading too many horror stories. The pod's lid clicked down with a whoosh of air, and the life support began increasing the soft pressure lining on the inside. Derric pushed his fingers down into the control gloves and tested the command buttons.

"We all in?" he asked Rodriguez.

"Aye, sir," was the reply, as expected.

"All right, get on the horn to Earth. Tell them we're ready for the jump." Derric clicked down the engine room button. "Rat, this is Derric. Are all your men stowed?"

"Aye, sir. I've got the cyborg stationed to keep an eye on that pump."

"Do you think it's that bad?"

"No, the safety margin is still in the upper eighties, but I'd rather we had something there just in case."

"Fine, but let me know if anything happens."

"You got it, sir."

Derric felt the pressure increase against his body. He punched up the view screen and read-outs. Rantson was right; the pump still operated in the green.

"Almost ready for jump," Rodriguez's voice cut in.

"Raise control again and tell them this is the last transmission before jump blackout."

"Yes, sir," the lieutenant responded crisply.

The light drive began kicking in, hurling the *Lancelot* forward on the wings of plasma backwash. The view screen in Derric's pod became a blazing array of colors. He squinted and pressed the automatic view adjuster. Suddenly, Derric was slammed with immense weight on his chest. He gasped for air, and the view screen fogged up with his hot breath. The pod adjusted for the mass displacement and then Derric could suck air again. The roar of the engines groaning against the ship was deafening.

The *Lancelot* exploded through the light barrier.

The colors on Derric's screen dissipated, leaving thin rays of light trying to play catch-up with the faster craft. Derric felt very much like he imagined the first test pilot of the late twentieth century whose feeble machine had just broken the sound barrier must have felt.

"Status," Derric huffed from his laboring lungs.

"All systems functioning, sir," Rodriguez said in a strained voice. "We're picking up heat. The coolant is up two hundred degrees."

Derric's intercom bleeped and he pressed the receiving button.

"Captain, there's definite heat buildup down here," Rantson stated.

"Can you get that cyborg on it?"

"Ah, no, sir. The jump tore him apart. There's nothin' left but a smear splattered on the bulkhead. We can't get to it until we slow below light speed."

"Time to deceleration?"

"Already in deceleration," Rodriguez answered. "Sublight in two minutes. We have a safety margin of five minutes to the end of the run corridor."

"You heard that, Rat. You've got less than five to cool this crate down."

"But Derric…"

"You heard me! We haven't tested the shields on the system plasma flow. Unless you want to litter the stars from here to Alpha Centauri, you'll get out of those pods and on it as soon as possible!"

"Yes, sir."

The stars fell twinkling by the wayside as the *Lancelot* bulled her way back through the light barrier. Derric felt relieved as fresher air circulated into the pod when the hatch finally blew open.

"Stations. Everyone to stations," he said as he stumbled through the opening to the command chair. "Get me a deep scan right now."

Rodriguez's fingers flew on the console and the scanners began to reach their probing pulses past the approved jump corridor.

"Beyond the safety corridor lies a dust cloud stretched out on an interstellar eddy."

Damn, thought Derric. Not a serious problem at sublight speeds, but a collision at this rate would rip through the deflectors, atomizing the *Lancelot* instantly.

Mission control had called this one too close. Derric looked down at the coolant temperature: One hundred seventy-nine degrees above—but stable and operable.

Derric tapped his fingers nervously. "Engine room."

"Sir."

"Status."

"Nitro pump at near 82.7 percent output. Just enough for a smooth deceleration." Rantson sounded relieved.

With deceleration on schedule, they'd make it with only a chip or two on the paint. Nothing would make Derric happier than sitting in the officer's club on Alpha Base, Titan, with a tall cool one in hand, telling other patrons how this was just another test flight. Just another test flight, like hell—the *Lancelot* made history breaching the light barrier, and the whole crew was now immortal.

"Decelerate, Lieutenant."

The engines whined, and the ship shivered. Light rays shot past the main screen while the craft slowed.

The red light by Derric's left index finger blinked on.

"Engine room, what's going on down there?"

"The nitro pump just blew the main seal! We've got to reduce power for the deceleration. Moving to redundant systems." Rantson breathed hard with the crew noisily working in the background.

"You milk all the resistance you can out of those engines, even if you have to melt them down!"

Rantson turned from the intercom to bark the orders to the engine crew.

"Captain, the power decline's going to take us to the fringe of the debris cloud," Rodriguez said. "Deflectors at full charge should push aside most of the particles at present rate."

A flair of light flashed across the screen. The ship quaked.

"We've got a major power loss!" Rodriguez raised his voice over the groaning hull.

"Engine room report!" Derric shouted into the intercom. There was no answer. "Report!" There was more silence before the reply.

"Captain, this is Assistant Engineer—"

"I don't care who you are! What's going on?"

"Sir, the nitro pump threw an internal bearing. We're switching on the secondary at 52.7 percent capacity."

"Rodriguez, give me the estimates."

"Yes, sir." The onboards whirled back the answer. "Captain, we won't reach suitable sublight until well into the cloud."

Derric punched up the information and looked at the figures. Sweat formed on his brow while his fingers painstakingly entered an access code. The computer cleared him, allowing for the completion sequence. The *Lancelot's* onboards began relaying stored data back to Earth via sublight transmission.

"Status on deflectors?" Derric queried.

"Deflectors on standby. Maximum charge available, but at present rate of deceleration they won't last more than two-point-five minutes."

Derric bit his upper lip. The dust cloud was becoming a visible swirling mass on the screen. Due to its enormous size and the *Lancelot's* speed, contact was unavoidable.

"Activate deflectors. Plot a course adjustment to the area of the least concentration. Maybe we can punch a hole through it."

The shields energized a soft glow about the ship's nose. The scanners scoped through the dust, returning information for the computers to chew on. The cloud did have a section with fewer particles per kilometer than the cloud as a whole. The onboards locked on and made the alteration. The *Lancelot* hurled on her perilous run.

The first wave of particles ionized in the shield's field. Blinding flashes sparked across the view screen. As more particles collided, the field glowed a sickly red.

"Step up the engine-braking resistance."

"Temperature is critical," responded the engine room.

"Just do as I say!" Derric yelled. If they had to blow the drive to slow the ship, then so be it. He pulled up the nav control and rotated the thrusters. He could not alter the trajectory, but if he could spin the ship and utilize the thrusters there might be a chance... He didn't complete the thought. He simply acted.

The onboards worked furiously, calculating to the microsecond where the shield was weakening and re-energizing those spots. Thrusters fired, moving the nose, and the motion rippled through the shields.

A particle of dust, small enough to be invisible to the naked human eye, passed through a minuscule opening. But a plasma burn incinerated it and punched deep into the cloud before the *Lancelot's* hurling mass hammered against it, sending the particle into the hull. The rotation continued, spinning the ship around at an agonizingly slow speed. More particles flamed against the shield, lighting up the view screens in a display of wild colors.

Derric monitored the heads-up display and adjusted the energy flow to the thrusters, pushing the output above the standard tolerances for the system. The main engines were already warmed up, so he eased the throttle to build up a burn that lashed out into the debris field, vaporizing chunks and particles in an instant. Elation swelled Derric's lungs when he sucked in the recycled air.

Steady burn—slow the ship and clear a pathway.

A single grain of dust slipped through the shield's regenerating cycle, and twisting metal disintegrated so fast the dead didn't have time to scream. Their remains were now scattered at just under lightspeed, across the dust cloud and into the cold void of space.

ΠAVIGATOR'S PRAYER

Holding sextant firm in hand,
my eyes to heavenward gaze.
I brace my feet 'gain heaving deck
astride the storming rage.
The mad seas crash the bow,
over the desperate creaking melody
of the strained timbers' protest.

Bleak, blackening clouds twist
rolling closer still, for thunder cracks
and lightning bursts with
fierce Odin's one-eyed wrath.
Many have weathered these wyrdded seas—
yet many more seasoned than I
deep drank her chilled grasp.

Where now, Ulysses, with rose-marbled gods,
to save from Sirens' songs?
Yes, trump them, Aeneas, with gilded voice, herald
of Dido's fall!

Virgil whispers not here
to guide through descending circles of gloom.
At point of the rocks, the beacon beams bright
as the breakers foam over my head.

THE CYBORG HEARTACHE

Manda shivered in the cold, squinting against the snow pelting her face, and picked up her pace along the frozen sidewalk. Leafless maple trees stood sentinel on either side, tall twisted specters that awaited spring for release from winter's icy bands. Manda pulled the insulated collar of her jacket up to her chin and smiled—for spring was just around the corner.

"Rand, Rand!" she shouted when she threw open the door. The warm air in the dwelling burst upon her, flushing her cheeks and nose red. "Oh, Rand." She rushed to her husband on the sofa. He looked up from the handheld vid screen and rubbed his face.

"What, dear?" he asked.

"I found him," Manda whispered and knelt next to her husband.

The corners of Rand's mouth drooped; his rough brow furrowed into steep rugged crags. "I thought we agreed to leave it be," he replied in a hushed tone. Sitting up, he switched off the vid screen and freed his eyes to meet Manda's. "You promised not to do this anymore."

"I know, I know. But remember the inquiries Sal promised to make with Central?"

Rand nervously ran his finger through grey-streaked hair, looking past his wife out the nearby window at the driving white that tinkered against the thermal glass.

"Of course I remember," he muttered. "I'm not sure I really want to know though."

Tears welled in Manda's eyes. "Please, Timos, at least hear me out, then decide."

Rand smiled slowly but raised a finger. "Remember, this doesn't mean yes."

Manda wiped her eyes and sat down next to her husband. "Okay, remember when I told you Sal could trace transfer invoices from the funeral home through the Cleveland Medical Cybernetic Division to the unit's final destination?"

Rand nodded slowly.

"Well, it took her a while to get around all the security codes without leaving tracers, but she finally located the plant where Jenal is."

"Geez, Manda, I've told you before, whatever they turned out, it isn't Jenal anymore."

"Oh, but it is, Rand." Manda sniffled. "It's still our son. I carried that body for nine months. Nine months! Then for seventeen years we loved him. He's our son!"

"Manda, he was our son. He died. Whatever they've done with the body, it isn't our business." Her husband brushed a tear from her cheek.

Manda looked away from her mate, warm, fresh tears replacing the one that wetted his fingers. She wiped them away and faced Rand again.

"Please hear all of what I've got to say. Please?" Manda's soft eyes pleaded more convincingly than her voice.

The frustrated man gave in. "Tell me."

"He's not far away, stationed at a Recycling Foundry in Erie. Sal says that he's been in the Decomp division since deployment, and he'll be there until he quits functioning. Please . . . please let me go see our son!"

"Damn it all." Rand's face turned pale. "You knew when we had Jen that if anything ever happened before he turned twenty-one, we'd have to give up the body to Cyborg Reclamation. Geez, Manda, we're not supposed to get this deep."

"I remember," Manda replied softly.

"You also remember the Third Child Contract we both signed before his birth?"

"Of course." Manda had tears running down her flushed cheeks. "And I've felt like Judas ever since."

"That doesn't matter now. He's dead. Whatever's working at that plant, it isn't Jen. His memory was completely erased and reprogrammed."

"But it's his flesh," Manda pressed. Rand looked away as she continued. "His heart still pumps the liquid. His nervous system controls the unit's functions. Can't you see, he is still part of me. part of you!"

Rand hung his head. Manda moved closer to him and affectionately ran her fingers through his hair. *This has been so terribly hard on him,* she thought. He didn't want a third child for exactly this reason. Poor

Rand, maybe she was pushing him a little too far. She pressed his head to her bosom.

"I'm so sorry," she whispered in his ear.

That night, Manda lay beside her sleeping mate, listening to his lively, rhythmic breathing. So many thoughts ran rampant in her mind, all centering around one solid idea: she knew where Jen was. Wet tears rolled down Manda's cheeks, the memories of the boy's funeral so painful. When she had pressed her hand against the cool view screen on the cryogen casket, Jenal's grey face had been so motionless. The only sound was the quiet hissing of the liquid nitrogen pumps shooting a cool mist over the corpse—keeping it perfectly preserved for future duties. Alive, she told herself, a part of him at least. His brain channeled signals through cyborg-augmented nerves controlling the organs regulating absorption of energy substances. Her son still lived; she knew it—the inexplicable mother–child bond. Manda hugged her pillow tight, finally able to feel a sense of relief that had eluded her for many long months.

The following morning dawned crisp and cold off the fresh snow. Manda didn't mention her thoughts of the night before as she shuffled Rand out to the bullet shuttle stop. She waved goodbye to her mate, smiling as he climbed the onboard steps, and breathed a sigh of relief when the shuttle pulled away with a jetting *whoosh* down the street. Rand wouldn't be able to catch the return shuttle until after six, giving Manda all day to turbo tram out to Erie and be back before dinner. She ran back in the house, grabbing her traveling bag from a chair, and then bolting out the back door. Mrs. Fenton gave her a ride to the tram stop in Old Mentor.

Snow crunched beneath Manda's boots as she stepped to the platform. The sky was greying, the outstretched wings of another storm rolling in off Lake Erie. Manda rubbed her hands together, briskly walking down a ramp into the station. Not many of the tram's passengers disembarked here. Erie, the city, had almost ceased to be these days, at least since the Environmental Reclamation Department founded the National Recycling Foundry. Decomp was the last division to start up and the one that sealed Erie's fate as a starving community. Radioactive and organic waste recycling had left a terrible mark on the city and its inhabitants.

Manda scurried to a shuttle, avoiding contact with the natives.

Dark buildings huddled along either side of the street as the shuttle whizzed around corners like a daring insect, cutting into the heart of town. Huddled forms, going about their business, shuffled down the sidewalks, their rags dragging in the dirty snow.

Must be some of the mutations still running around, Manda thought for a second, but she didn't dwell on them. She had her own worries.

The sun peeped timidly through the dark skies when Manda stepped from the shuttle to the steps of the Foundry Visitor's Center. The building was a smudged black, its tall columns reaching up like smokestacks on some of the abandoned steel mills in Cleveland. Manda ducked her head against the wind and ran up the entrance. Once she got on a tour of the actual plant, she hoped to catch a glimpse of Jen, but despite not knowing what he would look or act like, Manda knew she'd recognize him.

The dirty auto doors *whooshed* open to the foyer. Manda entered, shaking flakes of snow from her hair. Brushing the loose strands back, she looked around.

Dirty people crowded around the main visitors' desk, waiting for someone to check their personal IDs so they could get free tickets for the warm tour of the plant. Manda jostled in among the homeless, filthy, rag-covered residents of Erie's streets, whose only escape from the cold was a three-hour tour through the very cause of their city's demise. Manda shouldered closer to the desk. There were no visitors to be seen dressed in decent clothes except her. She'd been fortunate to marry a man with a job in the Malaysian Industrial Conglomerate's Customer Inquiry Office, and the yen they paid went a lot further these days than dollars.

A door opened up behind the counter and a man in a Government Services uniform emerged. He stepped up to a microphone, clicked it on with a squeal, and said, "Line forms up to the right." The clot of people bunched forward, Manda along with them. The housewife from the eastside of Cleveland merged with the mob, pressing to the only relief many of them would get all winter.

Manda pulled a flat personal ID from her coat pocket when she finally made it to the desk. Her stomach was nervously flitting butterflies as she handed the plastic card to the attendant and he slid the magnetic strip side through the reader. Not noticing the slight tremble in her lip, he asked her the standard declaration.

"Do you have relatives either employed for this facility, or in the cybernetic auxiliary?"

"No," Manda replied.

He nodded. "Thank you, Mrs. Starkey. Go ahead through the gate and join the tour group."

Manda smiled, took back the personal ID, and walked past the security scanners.

The attendant pushed the red security check light.

"Security here," said a voice in the console speaker.

"Yeah, this is the visitors' entrance. I think we might have a breach here. The cross-check flagged a visitor."

"What? Hold the person in the foyer."

"Too late, she's already gone through."

"You let this person through? Whattdya do a stupid thing like that for?"

"Cuz it's the first time I ever had someone try using improper ID to get in, that's why. This isn't a resort location!"

"Okay. I'll get a check on it."

Denton released the mic button and rocked back in his chair. He pulled his terminal keyboard out and began punching up the incident inquiries. Starkey, Sedora J. Production worker R. J. R. Inc., Euclid, Ohio. Punched in to work at 7:45 a.m. Checked in at the Foundry Visitors' Center 10:19 a.m. With a keystroke he accessed additional information from the government cross-files. A name came up as a link to Sedora Starkey: Manda Nelson, her first cousin, had used her own credit ID to purchase a round trip to Erie from Mentor, Ohio, Sedora's region of residence. The only round trip issued. Obviously, this woman thought to get away with someone else's personal ID without knowing a linkup existed with the national employers' reference system.

Manda stepped out onto the causeway. Far below the enclosed tube were the cold Erie streets. The narrow path rolled from the main visitor's center to the plant proper, and with each passing meter Manda was more at ease. Passing through on Sedora's personal ID certainly worked better than she'd thought it would. If she had used her own, they'd have easily crossed it with a cybernetic work list, catching her before she'd even started. Manda shuddered to think of the consequences for breach of contract with the government.

The auto doors at the end of the tube hissed open, and the group was moved on the conveyor belt into the dirty bowels of the foundry. Manda caught her breath at the sight of the huge machines, glowing and sparking with molten refuse. Hot cinders flew through the air, falling stars gone mad. Some hit the clear tour tube, expending them with a flash. Beyond the tubs and vats, dark figures scurried to and fro.

Below, the contingent of cyborgs manning the various stations appeared no larger than ants. Some of the cyborgs came close enough that Manda felt she could reach out and grab their corroded body plates, hoping to get the attention of one that had been her son. She sighed. Maybe Rand was right. There was no way she could ever hope to find Jen here.

"Psst!"

A skinny hand grabbed Manda around the elbow, and she found herself looking into a gaunt, desperate face. The man's bare cheeks were terribly marred by acne, and his scraggly facial growth hung about his chin in a sickly grin, but despite his appearance, Manda found she couldn't take her eyes from his.

"What, what is it?" Manda asked, her voice faltering a bit.

"Shh. It's okay," he said. "You ain't like the rest of us. Whatcha doin' here?"

"Just here to take the tour," she answered guardedly.

"C'mon," he pressed, squeezing Manda's elbow a little tighter. "You ain't from here; you're dressed too well. Besides, no one from out of town ever comes here, not even for a tour."

Manda tried pulling her arm free but couldn't break his grip.

"Who are you?" she whispered. "Why are you doing this? I've done nothing to you."

"Right enough," he said, raising a finger to his lips. "It's just ladies like you ain't never seen down here until they've been so used up they don't even look like ladies no more. So what are you doing here?"

"Just looking around." Manda's eyes darted back and forth, looking for an escape route. The people she was pressed against turned away, uninterested, and the smooth causeway tube continued on and on.

"Looking for what?"

Shivers ran up and down Manda's spine. If she was so transparent, everyone in the whole facility must know she was here for a reason.

"Would you just leave me alone?" Manda snapped at him. "It's none of your business!"

"You're right," he said, releasing her elbow.

Rubbing the joint, Manda moved away.

"It's okay with me if you get yourself killed," the man continued, mumbling. "It's a fine thing when you try helping someone and they spit on ya like you was trash."

Manda looked away. Outside the tube, cyborgs were loading large cubes of waste into furnaces. The tour guide's voice came over the speaker system to explain how the combustible waste provided enough energy to power the eastern United States and half of Canada. Not caring much, Manda continued squinting, trying to find Jen among the bustling mechanized dead working in the living's refuse.

The conveyor slowed to a stop as the group entered the Decomp area, and the tour guide's voice continued.

"Decomp is the finest product the human mind has conceived for waste disposal. In this department, organic materials are exposed to the same breaking-down processes as found in nature: water, heat, cold, bacteria, light, and wind, only intensified. The resultant organic compost is then packaged for freight to areas in need of soil construction such as Saudi Arabia, Egypt..."

A grinding noise to Manda's left caught her attention. One of the maintenance hatches in the side of the tour tube was being pried open by a large, rough-looking woman. She looked around, then slid down the dark opening, followed by others. Manda thought for a second. This was Jen's department, and a chance to get even closer might never come again. Bolstering some courage, she took a deep breath, looked around, and, since nobody seemed to care, bolted for the open hatch just as the conveyor jerked forward to continue the tour. Manda's hand slipped. She caught a slimy rung on the open ladder and stifled a cry.

The ladder was a lone metal pole, pegs extending from the tube to the foul-smelling grey mass far below. Manda could barely make out the shapes of those ahead of her. Realizing this wasn't the place to lose control, she gritted her teeth and began the descent. At the bottom, Manda stepped onto the corroded walkway only a few feet above the organic gunk. Before taking her first step away from the ladder, a hand reached around from behind her, clamping down across her mouth, successfully plugging up a scream.

"Shh!" hissed a familiar voice in her ear. "If you don't make any noise, I'll let you go. Deal?"

Manda had no other choice. She slowly nodded.

"Now," said the same man who had questioned her on the tour, keeping a secure arm around her narrow waist. "So what brings you here? This is no place for the suburbs."

"I can't, it's none of your business. I've already told you that."

The man spun her and tightened his hold. With a finger pointing in her face, he said, "Look, lady, this ain't your world in here. There's no white picket fences and rose gardens. If you don't tell me what's going on, I may as well just do what I want to you here, cuz you sure ain't gonna survive this place."

Manda turned her face, teeth clenched tight.

"Either way you'd be just as dead." The man moved his finger down Manda's already open coat to the top of her tunic.

"Okay," she whispered, not expecting the answer to do any good. She was as good as dead, and he'd leave her used body in the muck; she'd end up fertilizer in some farmer's underdeveloped field. "I'm here to find someone who died and has been through Cyborg Reclamation. When I saw the woman open the ladder to Decomp, it was too good to be true. I thought maybe I'd find him."

She squinched her eyes expecting the worst any second.

"Who's it you came after?" he asked gruffly.

"My son."

"You stupid, stupid woman!" The man released her, turning to spit on the walkway. "I can't believe you're even here."

"Well, I am," Manda said straightening her jacket. "Now if you'd just stop bothering me, I'll finish looking on my own."

The man laughed, a rattling sort of sound, shaking his head all the while.

"They take lots of shortcuts here in everything except internal security. They're on to you."

"Come on." Manda smiled weakly. "If they're on to me, how come you're here?"

"Don't you know, Mrs. Suburb?" he sneered back. "They tolerate us cuz we're not a threat to anything. The system always makes allowances for its own refuse. It's guilt. Besides, we've got no place to go and they know it."

"Well, I covered my tracks so they won't even know a member of the immediate family came here."

"It doesn't matter. They'll find out and take care of you."

"I'm here," Manda insisted, "and since I've got this chance, I'm going to take it. So either kill me or let me see if I can find my son."

The man narrowed his eyes, clicking his tongue against the roof of his mouth. "Hell, I never did have much sense," he moaned, throwing his hands up in a gesture of surrender. He extended a filthy hand to her. Manda took his hand into her own. "Just call me Verj."

"Okay, Verj. My name's Manda," she replied.

"I'll take you to the cyborg feeding station."

"What's there?" Manda asked, following his billowing rags down the causeway.

"It's where the 'borgs go to feed their human parts. That's why we're here. We get slop there. But remember, just stay low-key and don't talk to any of the 'borgs."

"What— Why?"

Verj spun around, glaring at her. She felt a shiver go up her spine as he gruffly spoke.

"Not only because I told you, but because if you do and they're on to you, we're both dead. You just don't understand, do you? It's not like your world here—it's not! If one of those 'borgs recognizes you... If the outside world knows the truth..."

"Recognizes me? My son won't even know my face from yours. They wiped his memory."

"That's what they told you." Verj clenched his teeth, grabbing her face in a hand. "This isn't your world. I've told you that, so don't act like it is. These 'borgs know who they are; I talked to a few. It's cheaper to leave 'em alone, then put the programs right in over the brain. They cut costs here. Geez, they cut costs all over this place!"

Manda's face lit up. She stopped listening to the rest of what Verj was saying. Jen might recognize her; he might know she was his mother. Her heart beat faster at the possibility her boy might still be alive and have control of his mental faculties.

Verj shook her. "You're not even listening to me, are you? Look, if you're seen and they already have a line on you, security might kick in and you'll be toast. Got it?"

Manda nodded. "Yeah, yeah, I understand."

"Man, there'd be one huge scandal if word got out you found your boy and actually spoke with him, eh?"

Manda said nothing. She just fell back in step with her guide, who led her to the next ring of the inferno, the ramifications of her visit just dawning on her. Violation of the government's third-child contract was a serious offense, but if the conditions of cyborg reclamation hadn't been met by the government or their contractors, not only was there going to be a serious scandal in the cyborg program, she might also get Jen back.

"She's not on the tour anymore?" Denton asked over the intercom of the attendant standing at the end of the tour. "Okay, wait a minute while I get clearance for a security code ten... That's right, security code... Uh-huh... Hang on."

"What? What's this about?" The secretary of Environmental Reclamation's voice rose with each word. "I don't want this to get out, Denton. Make sure! It can't get out of the department. We take care of our own, you know."

Denton cut the line and pushed his chair back. He hoped the conversation ended at the secretary level.

Security Unit 175A leaned over the food dispenser with a white organo-plastic cup in its hand. The nutritional material slopped in. The unit raised the corroded faceplate covering its grey, human face and gulped down the tasteless paste. After finishing, the creature carelessly flicked a drop of the stuff off a steel finger, focusing its targeting grid as the goop flew in a blob through the air. The unit moved down the line, past some shabby living humans, to the water dispenser.

"But I might be able to catch sight of him over there," the cyborg heard through an ear transceiver from one of the nearby humans. The man-machine's remaining human indifference passed from its mind to the computer interface for processing. It bent over and turned the dispenser knob to splash a stream of water in a sparkling cascade. The cyborg sucked the liquid.

Red glare hazed over the cyborg's optical screen, signifying a security system boot up, then code key for override. Unit 175A straightened up, watching the instructions dot the bottom of the screen with a brief message.

"Security breach—all security units in the Decomp alerted and engaged in enforcer mode. Suspect description 42 years of age, 5' 4", Caucasian female, brown hair, and brown eyes. Be advised she is dressed in well-kept clothes and is in the company of food leeches."

"Hmmm..." the cyborg half mumbled through scratchy speech synthesizers. The organic human brain wondered what this woman might have done to deserve enforcer mode code ten in the middle of the Decomp pit. Very few living creatures besides the leeches even dared descend into the grey, stinking decay. The cyborg wrinkled its nose out of reflex, even though its olfactory sensors were long used to the environment.

When the cyborg signaled for a visual identification, static was the only response. After one more attempt for a visual identification, the unit began looking over the area in its visual range. Nothing but the same old dismal surroundings, just some old rusty 'borg units and human leeches feeding at the dispensers. A crooked smile twisted its grey lips at the stray recollection of...

The cyborg relocked its optical sensors, and the unit felt its human lungs deflate.

"Mother..." The word barely passed the speech synthesizers through the cyborg's human lips, and the unit that had been Jen took a step forward.

"Watch out," Verj yelled, pushing Manda aside and pulling a rusty metal bar from inside his ragged coat. Manda watched in horror as the cyborg security unit they had been trying to avoid raised a steel-plated arm against Verj's sudden blow. The bar rang against solid plating and bounced off harmlessly. The unit grabbed the hapless man by the scruff of the neck, throwing him into the grey, organic muck beyond the feeding station platform. The grey behemoth turned, its faceplate open, to face the terrified woman.

"Jen!" she screamed, her voice shrill. "Jen, it's me! It's your mother!"

The cyborg staggered, its hands clutching its metal/flesh head. Jen's thin, grey face writhed in agony on its cerebral plate like a sizzling egg on a skillet, the creature's thick steel hands flexing dangerously, clanking the knuckle plates over the finger joints. Jen/175A tore at the security program, but the organic nerve sensors cut off his control over unit functions. Utterly helpless, the central computer began dictating the cyborg's movements.

"Maaaa!" he forced through the constricted vocal mechanism and, chained to the machine, watched 175A's actions in horror.

Manda wiped the tears from her eyes, her cheeks salty wet. She swept through the relief in her mind and into the arms of her strong son, her little Jen—her boy. Once in the cyborg's hydraulic clutches, the mother kissed her son's cool face. The steel-plated arms engulfed her and, with her dying breath cooing in his ear sensors, Manda gurgled thankfully for her son's solid embrace.

The woman's body went limp in the cyborg's arms as the metal and flesh creature pulled bloody fingers from around her waist. Through the distortion of the cleansing fluid around the optical sensors, Jen/175A looked down at his mother's pale face and screamed—screamed over the droning sound of organic refuse collectors harvesting the grey Decomp sludge.

Then, deep in the systems of control that were wired into his cervical cortex and that had been walled off from his body by the systems constructed to keep the Frankenstein under control, something stirred. A growth, a cluster of cells, a nerve—some might think them but random or an anomaly in a creature built for servitude. But stimulated by the very chemicals pumped into the dead flesh to keep it functioning, these new growths, these very new routes of nerves blossomed around the devices and the subsystems. A finger twitched of its own accord, then Jen gathered his mother into his arms and flung her into the compost, where her body would quickly break down and never be found.

THE DEMON'S DEPENDENCY

His eyes drank deep, my goblet
of pulsing veins, throbbing.
Those frigid eyes
of my living warmth did want
to feed the black flames.
Crooked fingers, jittering and nervous,
betrayed him, the golden
shafts of dawn soon piercing
shadowed night, and I
the last of human flesh
to wander barren streets.

He'd bled them all,
from each cup drunk deep,
dooming all to endless hell,
with days of restless sleep.
I the last, the only one,
held fast his fate,
for if he drinks till draught is done,
it will surely be his last.
Neither cross nor holy symbol
had stopped this fellow before, but
now he stood, still,
silent,

and I had one last breath,
for no matter how foul,
the deal needed be struck.
His eyes widened dangerously

at words so bold, thus I did repeat.
"Devil," I spoke, "tonight you've finally feasted,
and when I die your spirit will hie
to the unknown gloom."
Shaking, the beast's eyes faltered,
saliva drooled from his thin-lipped mouth, and,
for the first time in hundreds of years, he wept.
Sizzling tears hissed on the ground, spattering
the dirt with a sulfurous splash.
He wiped his stony face—
beaten was this creature
who'd drunk from a thousand springs;
now conquered by one.
"This just might work," he hissed,
"to benefit both. Mortal,
you yet shall breathe,
heart in flesh beat, never again
to fear death's cool touch."
Round me his rigored arm wrapped,
the cool comfortless leech,
and through the dismal streets
we strode,
the city of the dead.
Many's the night since, in
madness I cried
for the gilded shafts of light
that herald the great god's ride
through the unlimited expanse of sky.
Still I, rusty chained to stone
tick the day's steady passing.
He arrives again and after his feed
the whisper creeps into my ear,
"Come with me—come."
The oily fires in the smoking ring
burning round perdition's hole
have woven flames through my toes,

burning my spirit's feet.
The view of tormented hell
spans before me as I'm lifted
high on a bat's stretched wings,
my soul cringing in the deep regions
the living should not go;
and with the coming dawn
alone in my cell I sit,
horror bathing my crawling flesh
and the bargain filled.
I rue the long dead night the bargain struck
For I alone live.

GI SIGHTS

The slender cast-iron post lowered to the deer's shoulder, just below its neck. The shooter adjusted with the rear sight to level off the picture. The creature's wide brown eyes scanned the clearing while it sniffed the air. A gloved index finger moved from a horizontal safety position to lay gently on the black rifle's trigger. A mist of breath notably paused, the lingering puff dissipating above the charging handle. Even though a blanket of snow lay across the ground, that blanket already gave way to patches of dead grass and brackish mud.

One shot.

The deer flinched. Ellie let out her breath like a punctured balloon. She blew away a strand of dishwater-brown hair that fell across her nose from the knit cap pulled down about her ears. Then she drew in her breath once more. Held it. Ever so gently, she squeezed the trigger.

The shot cracked and the black, utilitarian .308 rifle bucked in the crook of her shoulder.

The doe staggered before dropping to its knees with a blossom of blood.

Ellie dared another quick breath, then held it.

But nothing moved in the undergrowth nearby.

She lowered the rifle, crawling to the edge of the deer stand that overlooked the field from the bole of a skeletal maple tree. She looped the rifle across her back and slid down the ladder to the ground. Once her feet hit the snow, she searched around the tree trunk until she found the spent brass, stuffing it into her pocket. She snatched up her backpack, then trotted through the section of cleared snow stretching between the tree and into the field to where the deer lay sprawled. Ellie gingerly stepped across the scraped ground—her boots placed carefully until she crouched near the fallen creature. From inside the pack, she pulled a wadded tarp and shook it out.

Her actions were practiced, almost mechanical. Though her fingers were stiff, they were efficient. With her skinning knife, she opened up the carcass and drew the sharp edge along the inside of the hide and the innards to field dress it. Once finished, she packed the carcass into layers of plastic, leaving a smear of blood and intestines in the already dirty snow. From inside her pack, she drew out a sack of brown pine needles and glops of tar. These she rubbed along the outside of the plastic, sniffing along the surface occasionally to test the pungent evergreen smell. Finally satisfied the task was complete, she straightened, stretching her back with a crack.

High above, the sun moved beyond noontime, the air warm and wet. With the fast-moving spring thaw, venturing this far from the barn was far more dangerous than fighting the snows in the dead of winter. Warmth loosened things better left frozen beneath, awaiting the change in the seasons.

She wove the rope into the tarp's grommets, then with the remaining length, she created a loop to slide her arms and shoulders through in an improvised harness. The lingering smell of burnt gunpowder bit her nostrils when she peeled off her gloves to scratch at her nose. After tossing pack and rifle onto the crude sleigh, Ellie quickly surveyed the fields. Satisfied with what she saw, she stuffed her gloves into her pocket, looping the rope over both her shoulders, then leaned into the load to begin the trek home.

After but a few minutes slogging through the muck, she gained the road. Snow yet covered much of the pavement where it had freely drifted during the winter and had now begun to melt. Not necessarily the easiest route, but she had scouted it during the early winter after the first few frosts had scattered ice across northeast Ohio. Now, she carefully followed her own footsteps in the crusted white—the same steps taken every time she had come to and from this field.

Step with care. She repeated that mantra over and over in her head while dragging the carcass around the accumulations and sliding over iced blacktop that had begun to appear in blotches. It had been years since a snowplow cleared these roads, after the snowstorm that preceded the outbreak. Amid the ensuing chaos, her parents navigated quarantine to steal her off to the family farm where she met up with her brother, newly returned from Afghanistan.

And there she remained.

The rope bucked against her shoulders upon crossing a wet, heavy drift of snow. But she kept her feet in the worn path—step after step after step. Upon reaching the nearby crossroad, she noticed vehicle tire tracks that swung onto the road across her path.

"Damn it," she muttered. Anyplace with other people was most certainly a place she did not want to be.

The tarp scuffed along behind until she reached the perpendicular dirt road where she would turn to the east, cutting through the fields, woodland, and gullies until reaching the small farm that had been her family's sanctuary for decades prior to the plague. About three more miles lay between her and the fenced paddocks surrounding the old red barn that had become her castle of solitude. Yet, the vehicle tracks continued straight ahead along the paved road.

She paused, shielding her eyes from the glare glancing off the snow.

The tire tracks tore through a drift and took a sharp turn toward the house laying just over a small rise in the road. A slender spout of steam rose above the snow drift. Beyond that drift, the chatter of voices reached her.

Ellie sloughed off the ropes, grabbing her rifle, the blackened steel cold in her hand. With her index finger, she clicked off the safety. The smell of gun oil and spent powder was familiar, and that gave her a modicum of confidence.

She cleared her throat, for she hadn't spoken to another human being for a very long time. Then she said, "Hello?"

While the chatter continued, she could now make out distinct voices. But no one responded to her.

"Where will we go?" someone asked. "The hospital is miles away."

"It could be a hundred miles away," replied a gruff voice. "But we have to get Tom someplace to stop that bleeding."

Ellie took a step into the tire track, carefully glancing at the snow on either side before she took another.

Always step carefully in the snow. She repeated over and over, urging herself to measure and gauge each placement of her foot. Her boot slipped on the ice that lined the track, causing her heart to leap. She steadied herself with a slight twist of her right ankle, gathering the rifle back to the ready. She wished nothing more than to turn down the nearby dirt road.

"Hello?" she called louder this time, her index finger trembling above the trigger of the rifle.

"Who's there?" that gruff voice challenged.

Upon rounding the snow, she came face-to-face with the occupants of an ambulance that lay buried in a white wall and spattered in muck. The double doors were thrown wide with faces crowding the opening. Two men in blue uniforms crouched near the prostrate form, blood staining the blotched snow.

Within the vehicle, some of the passengers appeared attached to medical gear.

Ellie lowered her rifle.

"You all right?" she asked, not yet willing to allow the rifle to drop completely from her hand against the sling.

One of the men met her eyes, concern creasing his face. "We were transporting patients to the county hospital, trying to beat the thaw." The man's voice was gruff, but it cracked slightly with emotion. "Goddamn it . . . he plowed through these drifts. You know, use the weight of the bus to get through."

"He's hurt bad?" Ellie asked.

The man bent over the stricken driver wiped at his eyes with one of his hands, then looked up. "We need shelter . . . where we can stop the bleeding."

"You have supplies? Blankets?" Ellie asked.

The gruff voiced man stood up. He was taller than Ellie, and his dark hair framed his concerned face. "This was to be a one-way run. Straight to the hospital, no stops."

"Well, you stopped," Ellie observed wryly. She glanced at the open door of the bus. "How many? And how long?"

"Right to the point," the taller man replied. "Ten patients and four staff. Our hospital will be undefendable after the spring thaw. Management evacuating us to the hospital near here."

"How long? You know, until someone comes to help you."

He chewed at his lower lip.

"We radioed ahead, but we're still too far away for a signal to our mobile unit. Could be hours or days."

"The snow is melting." Ellie frowned. "The pavement will melt first. I don't know what's under all this."

"He doesn't have long if we don't stop this bleeding," said the man kneeling next to the driver.

"There's a house over there." Ellie pointed at the nearby four-square house set back from the road, its shape muted by dirty white siding.

The standing man surveyed the house, scratching at his chin. "We'd have to clear it first." He glanced at Ellie with a forced smile. "And you can lower that. We've got one pistol and a fourteen-round magazine. It's not intended for you."

The farm, while still a hike down the dirt road, was close and, following her own tracks, she could be behind the paddock gates with the tractor reinforcing the barn door in another hour or so. A few hours later her deer would hang in the smoker shed erected by her grandfather and which she used only in the winter to avoid trouble.

She took a deliberate step backward.

"Have you cleared a house before?" Ellie asked.

He shook his head. "Been at the hospital facility in Madison since the outbreak."

"I can help," Ellie stated with a flat voice. "But I have to get home. Can't stay."

"Fair enough," he said. "Mark. By the way, my name is Mark."

"Ellie," someone else said.

And there in the bus doorway stood a young man teetering with crutches, an IV line stretching from his arm to a clear bag on a hook near his head.

She squinted, focusing her attention on him.

"Is that you?" she asked, her voice not betraying her thoughts or emotions.

The youth, however, allowed a smile to cross his face, extending to his tired eyes.

"Of course, it's me," he said wryly. "I'm not sure how to be anybody else."

Ellie thoughtfully tucked a pinch of hair behind her ear.

"The weather's changing," she observed.

Her eyes swept the nearby home, a simple structure with a large freestanding garage next to it. Up the side of the garage, a staircase rose to the attic space above where before the outbreak, friends would gather, jamming to their parents' 1980s soundtracks and playing Dungeons and Dragons far into the night. No video games. Just storytelling with dice clattering across the tabletop as the final arbiter. Ellie bounced the .308 in her hands. But the van held people in wheelchairs. And even Sammy, the young man on crutches, would struggle up the long run of stairs to reach it.

"Who can check the house with me?" she asked.

The medical technician, Mark, raised his hand like an awkward schoolboy.

"I can help," he said.

She examined him in his dark blue jacket and pants, a light-blue collared shirt about his neck. He reached into the van and snatched out a crowbar, smacking it in the flat of his hand.

"I'll leave the gun with them," he said with a shrug. "Thought we'd be safe until a thaw, right?"

"Watch it," she warned. "Step where I step."

She slipped the weapon sling from over her head and pointed the barrel to the ground. Poking at the snow until she was sufficiently assured, she took a step toward the driveway, already a patchwork with exposed blotches of asphalt. She leaped to land on one of those. The technician followed and made the short hop to the damp blacktop.

"See," he said with a grin. "Piece of cake."

Following the asphalt until reaching the snow once again, she aligned her approach with the house side door, and the rifle barrel once more broke the snow before she stepped. Another probing and she stepped again. While his face spoke of impatience, Mark followed, foot to footprint. After a few such careful steps, he placed his boot where her foot exited. His boot slipped on ice, but he quickly righted himself.

"Careful," Ellie snarled.

"I am, I am…" Mark replied with that lopsided grin. "I mean . . . how could any of this be a problem out here in the boonies?"

A glance from her and he clamped his lips together, then once more placed his foot into her trailing print punched in the heavy snow. Carefully, he shifted his weight, waiting for her to proceed another step farther. Her motions were assured, each movement precise, and the tap of her rifle barrel considered.

Above them, clouds deepened from blue to grey to purple with the sun cutting across the lower sky to the west.

The wind whispered warm across the fields.

At the door, Ellie placed a boot on the edge of the bottom step, brushing the next step with her toe. When she reached the front door window, she rubbed at the glass and stood on tiptoe to look inside. Shadows scattered from the doorway across the room to the sofa on the far wall.

"Looks clear," she observed, wrapping her fingers around the door latch. She turned it, but it held firm.

"We break it down, or something," Mark said over her shoulder.

Instead of attempting to force it, she kicked at the snow until she uncovered a floor mat, then bent and dug until she peeled the corner off the step. A key lay embedded in ice. She scratched at it with her fingers then held it up with a shadow of a grin.

"Might have to lock it later," she said.

But when she tried the key, the mechanism fought her. Ellie shook the doorknob. It remained stuck.

Mark reached around her.

"Let me try..." he started.

Then he slipped, falling off the step and into the snow piled beneath the eaves.

A grey hand cracked the icy crust, fingers grabbing at the EMT's arm.

"What the hell?" he yelped, flailing for the wrought iron stair rail.

"Watch where you place your hands," she snapped, reaching to grab his jacket then leaning back to pull him upright.

But the steel grey hand pulled at him. The snow behind him crunched and bent.

"Get up," she urged him. "Dammit, get up!"

A ruined face, crusted with ice and grime, exploded from the snow.

"What?" Mark blurted out.

She braced her feet against the rail and pulled.

The face lunged short of its prey. It raged against the ice layer beneath the snow.

Mark twisted around, snatched up his crowbar, then smashed the creature's hoary skull in a spatter of black fluid and grey brains.

"What were you thinking?" Ellie said, each word sharp and stabbing.

His face flushed. "Just trying to help," he replied haltingly. "Sorry."

She let go of his hand.

"Stupid dies," she said bluntly.

She reached into her pants pocket and pulled out a lighter. She struck it, then held it against the door lock. After a moment, she inserted the key, turning it in the lock without a hitch.

She pushed on the door. It stuttered against something then jammed.

"Now can I help?" Mark asked with a humble note in his voice.

Carefully stepping to the side, she gestured to the door.

Deep down, she didn't totally blame the EMT or the others for their clumsiness. Within the hospital confines, they had been safe and secured while the epidemic swept through northeast Ohio. Those remaining outside the walls were cast adrift in a violent, hungry world inhabited by those who were infected but asymptomatic, others with runny noses and fever, and those who succumbed in both life and death. The dead preyed on those who thought they had escaped infection.

Mark hammered the door with his shoulder. It shuddered. He braced his boots this time, leaning against it until it creaked then bumped open. Around the widened door, desiccated hands clawed at his jacket, a gurgle bubbling from ruined lips. A shadow stumbled into view—prune face and milky eyes framed by thinned locks of black hair. Jaws snapped sluggishly, broken teeth grinding amid the black maw. Ice crumbled from the sides of its mouth.

"Oh, God," Ellie groaned.

This shambling beast was the very same young man who hosted their adventures above the garage into the long hours of the night, a gentle soul who attended the local college while living with his family.

The EMT raised the crowbar, but Ellie grabbed his arm.

"No..." she said with a hitch in her voice. "I've got this."

She drew her hunting knife from the scabbard on her web belt then squirmed between Mark and the doorjamb. The creature garbled unintelligibly. The knife flashed, plunging into the side of its head, ichor oozing from the wound around the blade. She yanked it free and the creature crumpled like a marionette with its strings cut, hitting the floor with a thump. Ellie stepped over the twitching corpse to search the remainder of the home, leaving the EMT alone at the doorway.

In the kitchen, his parents lay sprawled across the table, heavy kitchen knives protruding from their skulls. She covered her mouth. When he reached her side, the EMT dragged the bodies to the mudroom at the back of the house, pulling the door closed behind him.

Clouds thickened overhead, a swirling late winter storm blowing in on the wings off Lake Erie. The maples of the surrounding wood bent to the touch of that wind, branches wildly twitching and snapping. While the group aided the patients from the bus, raindrops marched across the fields. In years past, this was the time of year for tapping trees, hanging buckets, and collecting the precious sap to be boiled into a sweet syrup, once a treasure for residents of the region. Now the trees groaned and creaked as silent specters before the heavy clouds.

The medical personnel carefully gathered their patients in the living room under Ellie's watchful eye. Then they lugged equipment that might be needed for patient care until the hospital might send aid. Mark loosened the vehicle's battery, wiring and cables, and the radio. Once inside, he dropped them next to the medical equipment. Ellie shut the door, throwing the latch with a solid *thunk* from the dead bolt.

"Will they find us here?" an older woman asked, concern in eyes surrounded by wrinkles and white hair. From her nostrils hung a line of oxygen strung to a canister beside the recliner where she had been deposited.

In the days before the pandemic, her friend's father often sat in that same chair, a tall homebound gentleman with white hair who wheezed and struggled without his own oxygen canister. Years of smoking had left him in the vulnerable population when the pandemic hit the Midwest. With his emphysema-ravaged voice, he often regaled her with stories of her grandparents and the history of the nearby hamlet laying amidst Ohio farmland—a crossroads town with a mom-and-pop grocery, a dilapidated television repair store, and an antique shop. Now this same man lay in a heap in the mudroom with his wife and youngest son.

Ellie wondered about the rest of the family but pushed the thought aside. Such dalliances were pointless, for the virus had been no respecter of persons, cutting down the wealthy, the poor, the old, the young, those who refused the vaccine, and some who accepted it. However, at death, the virus consumed all when immune systems failed, and bodies rose with renewed, ravenous life.

Suddenly, the air in that small home suffocated her.

The youth sat on the sofa, his saline bag hanging from the nearby table lamp. He followed her with his eyes, a lopsided grin on his scruffy cheeks.

She blew out a breath through pursed lips and walked over to him.

"It's good to see you," he said, adjusting the glasses perched on his nose.

She sat on the floor a few feet in front of him, crossing her legs beneath her. Her heart pounded in her throat. She swallowed hard.

"El, it's me," he said, a hitch in his voice.

"I know," she replied, rocking back and forth. "Why are you with, you know … at the hospital?"

"Cancer. I know, I'm too young."

"We thought we were too young for a lot of things," she said, nervously tucking a strand of hair behind her ear. "And now here we are."

Sam Burnett leaned forward—his brown eyes transporting her to another time. Many summers of youth camps, backyard football, and church barbeques had cemented his place as one of her most cherished childhood memories. She had considered his parents and siblings part of her own family.

"Your mom and dad?" The words escaped her lips. In the pit of her stomach, she knew his answer would further chip away at any thought that world could ever return.

Heavy raindrops pattered against the window at his back.

"Haven't seen them since chemo started. Shortly after, the quarantine orders came. I called every day until phone service went down. When they fortified the hospital, only supplies were allowed in." He turned toward the window and the road beyond.

A chasm of experiences had fractured their lives in the time that passed since the virus burned through the heartland along with failing antivirals, a vaccine that proved partially effective, and walking dead that now plagued the land with horrific, primal violence.

"Remember Sunday school?" Ellie whispered. "I miss Sister Edwards's class... She was so kind. And we got into so much trouble."

"Samuel Burnett..." He snorted. "You know the Lord has a plan for you. Made me shut up every time."

He closed his eyes and leaned back into the sofa.

"Are you in any pain?" Ellie asked.

He answered with a shrug. "Almost finished chemo before the meds ran out. The tumors on my spine are nearly gone. I can walk now. More every day."

A gasp from across the room where the EMTs crowded the stricken driver caught her attention. Ellie reflexively reached to her belt, wrapping her fingers around the knife hilt. The driver was dying, and then his immune system would fail. She scrambled to her feet, then crept up behind them. Illuminated by their flashlights, the driver's face was a deathly grey pallor.

Mark took his pulse and another EMT read the label on a syringe before pushing it into the driver's chest. Death swirled about them in the air.

"Note the time," Mark said.

The driver's body shook uncontrollably—his eyes rolled back to expose the whites, which were a bloodshot ruin. Saliva and blood foamed from his mouth.

"Did you hit him with antivirals?" Mark asked.

The other EMT nodded. Then Mark pulled a long surgical blade from an equipment pack.

"He's crashing," he snapped. "Cover us with that blanket. Please, pull it over here."

The other EMT grabbed a grey surplus, throwing it over them. With surgical efficiency, Mark bowed his head and mumbled a few words. Then he thrust the blade into the driver's temple, twisting it back and forth before jerking it loose. He drew the blanket over the now-still body.

Ellie looked away, and Sam's quizzical expression caught her eye.

"What?" she asked, smoothing her voice as best she could.

Sam could be a bit enigmatic, but she had never minded, for it caused her to consider her words with precision. And sometimes with humor.

"Do you still believe?" His question hung in the air as if it required an answer, yet the look on his face made plain it did not.

After all this time, there had been no time for reflection, and yet her faith had always been quietly below the surface of her reality. She thoughtfully pressed a few strands of hair from her eyes and shrugged.

In the early morning hours, a strong wind blew, and bare tree limbs scratched across the windowpanes. The rain had petered into a drizzle, blanketing the muddy grey landscape with a thick haze. Ellie, curled in a corner around the .308 rifle, had slept restlessly, her dreams littered with images of those she had lost. Her brother was among them, a tall, square-jawed young man who had served multiple tours in Afghanistan in the days before the first victim dropped dead near villages sprinkled among the Himalayan foothills.

On a distant morning last fall, Charlie left the farm hideaway, leaving her stomach tied up in knots in those first hours. He was her rock and her strength after losing track of her parents. Ever dutiful, he had remained through self-quarantine on the farm, then he made periodic runs to the local store to gather supplies and seek information from other survivors. But that morning would be the last she saw him, wrapped in his final embrace.

And then he was gone.

She stirred when the thump against the siding changed, became more substantial. With one hand, she brushed her loose hair from her face and with another, snatched a ball cap from her nearby pack. She shook it out, then pulled it over her hair.

"Always liked to play ball, didn't you?" Sam asked.

"Never the same since they traded Kipnis and Kluber," she muttered with a grin.

Something solid cracked against the outside of the house near her elbow. She raised her head above the window for a quick look. From the soupy fog they shambled, the dead emerging from their hibernation.

"Close the windows," she hissed. "Close anything that's opened."

Crouching low, she hurried to the front door, where she checked the deadbolt. Something scratched on the other side and rattled the door in the frame. She snatched back her hand.

One of the patients gasped.

Ellie raised her finger to her lips. Around them the others stirred, and she extended the gesture to each of them in turn. Fear spoke in their eyes, but they remained silent.

Mark crawled from a corner.

"What is it?" he whispered.

"Something hitting the house," she hissed back, her voice barely audible. "Thawed out overnight when the temperature rose."

The EMT appeared confused.

"They can hear us," she whispered. "Shut off anything that makes noise on that equipment."

He gave her a quick nod in acknowledgment then checked on the devices. She overheard him say to one of his colleagues, "... and no surprises."

She slid across the carpet to the west wall that overlooked the front yard and the street before the house that ran north and south. Nearby lay an open field that straddled the crossroads—a dirt road that led to the farm. She peeked over the edge of the windowsill.

Milky eyes met hers; inky ichor oozed from tear ducts deep in the rotting sockets. That lost stare chilled her lungs. She clenched her teeth, steeling trembling limbs against the urge to flee. She nervously reached for the knife at her belt with one hand while fighting the urge to fiddle with a loose strand of hair tickling her cheek with the other. But her eyes did not leave the creature's, and her breath trickled through her nose.

Moments passed before Ellie lowered herself beneath the windowsill, but now the wall erupted with flesh against clapboard, *thump, thump, thumping*. Black liquid and grey skin spattered against the window.

"What happened?" Mark gasped.

Grabbing the rifle, she slung it over her shoulder, then she jabbed a finger toward the kitchen. Sam glanced toward the window when they passed and coughed nervously when the large pane trembled. Those same eyes that rose barely above the sill caught sight of him. He sank into the sofa cushions.

Ellie skidded the kitchen.

"You have to call the hospital," she said to the EMT. "They are coming down the dirt road across the highway."

"We tried last night," Mark replied. "No one answered."

Her eyes swept the first floor, but what she sought wasn't there.

"My friend's dad talked with truckers on a CB radio base station," she said.

She crept to the sink counter beneath the kitchen window, reaching up and pulling the curtain aside. This window stood higher than the front room window, overlooking a sidewalk to the garage. Rising above the garage roofline stood a tower topped by a television, as well as a large radio antenna.

"Can we power that with the battery packs?" the EMT hissed through his teeth.

"I'm not too techie," she said, her eyebrows knitting together.

She returned to the living room, quietly exploring the desk near the hallway. The radio no longer sat near the old computer where the dials had once glowed. The connecting wires to the antenna had been pulled from the wall.

"Radio is gone," she hissed.

She gestured to Sammy, the most techie of their friend group. He acknowledged her with a nod then crawled from the sofa, grabbing his saline bag and tucking it under his arm. His movements were slow, and a bit stiff, but he crossed the distance on all fours. At the desk, he took the wires into his fingers.

"Looks like someone needed them for something else," he observed, examining the desk. He pinched a few plastic slivers between his fingers and rolled them around. "Look through the house."

Ellie quietly creaked up a narrow staircase. She quickly scanned the tumbled upstairs but found nothing related to a radio. Then her gaze caught a nearby window overlooking the garage. Beneath it, a gaggle of dead jerked, stuttered, and shuffled. Across the way, the radio tower stood above the roofline, the antenna reaching out like a centipede. Wires looped down from the tower. Her eyes followed them, but they didn't return to the house. From an overgrown thicket, a single strand of orange rose up the corner of the garage wall closest to the home and tucked under an upper window.

Power, she thought. Beneath the overgrown shrubs lay a generator partially buried in the snow that appeared sufficient for the garage. She hurried to the staircase and gestured to the EMT.

"Noise," Mark murmured. "Start that thing and the lower level of the house isn't safe."

"Bet the radio is up there," she said, pointing to the upper garage windows.

The stairs creaked and Sam teetered a bit before making his way to the window and peering out. He shrugged off her hand when she reached out to steady him.

"That is a mess waiting to happen." Sam gasped a bit, out of breath.

"Yeah," Ellie agreed. "But not today."

She trotted down the staircase, the rifle slapping her back. They could not refuge in the house much longer or they would have to put down the very patients the crew fought to transport before the thaw. Besides, this herd shambled in from the suburbs, heading toward the narrow dirt road—her dirt road.

"Can you get that thing working?" she asked Sam when he landed in the living room.

Sammy nodded, his face pale and his eyes dark. "If that thing runs, I will deliver."

"And you plan to clear all those things how?" Mark hissed. "We'll be chewed up in minutes . . . no, seconds, if we try dragging everyone to the garage."

"There's tools in there," she said. "And the antenna will get you a signal to the hospital. That's all you need. If there's still pressure in the gas lines, you have power."

Rubbing his stubbled cheek for a moment, Mark's face fell into thought.

But she didn't have the luxury of navigating doubts. That herd would destroy her refuge—the home her grandparents died defending. Charlie had kept that same farm safe by hunting strays that emerged through the wetlands and surrounding woods. No beast or monster had stood once captured in the GI sights of the .308.

"Do you have a flare gun?" she asked the EMT. "Any noisemaker will work."

"No. No way," Mark blurted out.

She rifled through the drawers in the kitchen, pulling out some of the heavy, long kitchen knives and tossing them into her backpack.

"Flare gun," she repeated to the EMT, holding out her hand. "You got one?"

With a grimace, he dropped to the floor, then crawled to the jumbled gear. The noise Mark created by rummaging through the gear was a painful to Ellie's ears. But once the EMT finished, he crawled back to her and handed her a sack.

"No flare gun," he whispered.

She opened it and inventoried the contents, then she tied it to her own pack. She gave Mark a thumbs-up.

"Don't start that generator until they're pretty far down the road," she said to Sammy.

He bobbed his head, but the whimsical look drained with the realization that her unspoken plan was already in motion.

"Don't die," he choked.

"I won't if you don't," she said.

They pressed their foreheads together, then parted.

She fumbled in the bag for a canned bullhorn, then stuffed it into a cargo pocket in her tactical pants. With efficient movements, she counted ammo magazines and rounds and pulled the charging handle on the black rifle with a deep metallic snap, feeding a round into the chamber. Then she tugged on her gloves, flexed her fingers, and wrapped the rifle sling about her neck—all the while a quiet prayer forming in her mind to be exhaled on her lips.

Her skin crawled along the back of her neck as if those earlier milky eyes still followed her every step. Ellie crept to the mudroom. Beyond the door, her friend and his parents lay in a jumbled heap. Covering her mouth with one hand, she carefully stepped between them. A grey hand fell across her ankle and she jumped, kicking one of the corpses and stumbling to grab the outer doorknob for balance. After a brief count of heartbeats, she snatched a stubborn strand of hair that tangled across her cheek and tugged it behind her ear. She opened the door, and a handful of dead greeted her with awkward, aimless shambles through the backyard. Beyond these few, Ellie knew there was no certainty once outside.

She took that step anyway.

Warm air nearly mugged her when she sprinted across the backyard toward the house next door to the south. The herd congregated at the front of the house like a bow wave on a ship riding through flotsam.

She sprinted to the neighboring blacktop driveway, then reached into her pocket and smashed the airhorn button with her thumb. It blared a bellowing clarion. The dead jumbled and jerked in confusion. She never truly understood what senses remained to them, but the noise attracted them like feral rats after the pied piper. With another sweep of her gaze to ensure her escape route, Ellie let loose another blast, this time longer. A gurgling and scraping closed behind her. She jogged down the driveway, pursuing calculated steps around snow.

At the main road, the long stretch of two-lane asphalt rose to the distant crossroads where the local store stood alongside the church, an elementary school, and handful of buildings—the totality of this midwestern town.

Waaaa... Waaaa... the horn spat out.

If there were dead closer to the town, they most certainly shambled to greet her. Ellie ran between the thick drifts, her boots deep in the slush pooling in the road. An arm extended from one drift, its hand wriggling the fingers upward toward the warmth while the creature's body remained buried in the deep, wet slope.

Waaaa... Waaaa... The trump echoed, and the herd swung sluggishly from the house, as more drifted across fields and roads toward her. She caught her toe on something in the shallow snow but adjusted and pressed on, playing the ugly note that sounded more like the horns of the damned than a call from a long-forgotten sporting event.

Waaaa... Waaaa.... She ran across a stretch of pavement, her boots leaving prints in the thick slush. She danced away from a nearby driveway where another dead dragged a lame leg, its arm twitching and slapping at its side. Ahead, a dead woman in a faded winter jacket, torn jeans, and winter boots sashayed in the middle of the street. Behind her followed more creatures in motley seasonal wear, attire that depended on when they succumbed to the virus.

She raised the rifle barrel just as Charlie had drilled into her, tucked into her shoulder while her pace slowed, more deliberate. She needed a path, and everything through the picture of those GI sights came into sharp focus. The cast-iron post lay in the center of the dead woman's head. Ellie lowered the gun slightly, then squeezed the trigger. The rifle bucked against her shoulder, the woman's face exploding into a ruin. Without hesitation, Ellie sighted her next target. When she pulled the trigger, her boot slipped on a patch of ice. The bullet ripped through the animated body in an explosion of guts and inky fluids. No pain crossed the creature's emaciated face.

However, Ellie fell with a stab of pain shooting through her knee and radiating into her leg. She cried out.

But the dead continued coming, twitching hands rising from its side, jaws gnashing with an audible clacking. Ellie scrambled, her rifle falling from her hands to swing by the cord about her neck. Her hand fell to the knife at her belt, pulling it from its scabbard with a rasp. Ellie lunged upward, driving the knife through an oozing eye socket into the creature's brain. The corpse crumpled atop Ellie before it finally stilled. She jerked the knife free, crawled away of the body. But another dead hurried along ahead of her, cutting across a muddy yard.

This one wore a weathered army jacket of digital desert camouflage.

"Charlie?" The word stuck in Ellie's throat.

But this corpse was too short, with a balding pate, weathered and grey.

It closed in on her—face twisted with ruined lips drawn back from blackened teeth, mouth slavering in dark gobbets. Ellie limped toward him, stabbing her finger at the name tape above a dark-stained hole in the garment—what could only be a bullet hole.

"That's my brother's, dammit," she growled, grabbing the knife in both hands.

Hobbled by pain, she lunged awkwardly at the creature, driving the knife under the creature's chin. It grabbed at her, jaws riding up and down the blade, but she held on, pushing the knife deeper until the dead crumpled to the pavement.

"You stole that..." Her voice faltered. "Damn it, you took it... You took my brother!"

The knife refused to come free from where it lodged. About her, more dead shuttled from the underbrush along the road ahead of her. And behind, the herd had finally begun to follow along the road, spilling into the adjoining fields. With the rifle stock, she crushed the desiccated face and hobbled onward. Her heart pounded in her chest while anger gave way to the realization that she could no longer outrun or dodge the emerging dead. The rifle rose once more. But the GI sights were no longer carefully targeted. The first of the dead crumpled in half when the round cut through its rotten gut to the spine. She smashed the rifle stock through the next creature's crusty skull, then dragged herself forward when the body pitched to the side.

Pain jolted through her knee, the joint threatening to fold beneath her.

"No," she growled through clenched teeth.

A glance over her shoulder revealed that the momentum of the herd had slowed.

Waaaa... Waaaa... The sound echoed across the road. She released the button and fought to keep herself upright. The scrape, scrape, scraping of feet grew louder. But she pushed on, focusing on the placement her feet, stepping carefully, and skirting the dead emerging from the winter's long hibernation. The stabbing pain remained a constant reminder that she was but another misstep from her knee failing.

The hamlet lay at the crossroads of two preinfection thoroughfares.

One road extended east to west, from the border of Pennsylvania to the suburbs of Cleveland, the other from Lake Erie in the north to the village of Parkman to the south—a small burg consisting of a small brick church, an elementary school, and a clutch of older homes. Between the park and the homes lay a country store, paint peeling from the old clapboard siding. Ellie limped across a stone sidewalk toward the general store where she planned to shelter with the family that had provided supplies to the surrounding area since the beginning of the outbreak.

But she halted near the center of the park and before the World War I memorial that rose above dead flower beds. Strung up in the middle of the column was a man—a man with a hole in his chest. Ellie couldn't breathe, for even though the grey skin was weatherworn, the dog tags dangling on his dead flesh screamed his identity. His head was stretched upward by a rope, milky eyes directed to the sky threatening rain. His jaw ground closed, then opened and closed again.

Ellie stumbled, her pack and rifle suddenly a stifling weight about her body.

The babbling grumble of the mindless dead followed her, and Ellie knew she needed to find shelter. As much as it pained her, Charlie would remain bound to the cold stone until she could free him. She shrugged off a shoulder strap then slid her pack around. From inside, she drew out the kitchen knives, sliding one into her web belt and another into her boot, pulling her cargo pant leg over it. In her hand, the carver felt like a boat anchor. But she could not risk a rifle shot drawing the crowd toward her. She ducked behind the overgrown landscape toward the general store where she sought both shelter and answers.

At the edge of the overgrown park's shrubs, she crouched and scanned the store. The building appeared quiet. She hobbled to the side of the building, where she peeked over the edge of a window. Shadows obscured the interior and light glowed through a doorway from another room. Not a flickering light, like a candle or oil lamp. Rather it appeared to be a digital glow, such as from an appliance. Ellie crept away from the entrance, glancing down at the blackened basement windows. At the back of store stood a solid, locked door.

Ellie crawled back to a nearby basement window, pulling her flashlight from a cargo pocket. She switched it on, angling the light into the window toward the floor to limit the scope and potential for the beam to be detected from the staircase. With her knife under the edge of the window, she pried at it until she heard a mute squeal of metal and a popping sound. She pressed her back against the sandstone foundation and waited for a moment or two before returning her wary eyes back to the window. Nothing within her field of vision appeared to stir. She lifted the window and leaned in, shining her light once more to the floor.

Then time ran out.

A creature rounded the corner of the building. Ellie shrugged off the pack and lowered her gear inside the window. Grabbing the awkward knife from her belt, she crept toward the dead. It sensed her in that strange way all the dead appeared aware of the living, whether from sound, smell, or sight. The hairy man's jaw opened wide in the bird's nest bushy beard, exposing a mouth punctuated with missing and shattered teeth. One of his arms swung limply, a weather-worn jacket torn and loose about an emaciated body.

Pain shot through her knee when she launched at the creature. Dragging her leg to remain upright, she fought to keep the dead's clawed hands from her face. The knife tumbled from her fingers to land near her boot. Ellie dropped to the ground, and the corpse tumbled over her. She crawled after it, driving the blade into the back of the creature's head. Wrenching it from side to side, she jerked it out before the corpse finished twitching. She scrambled to the window, slipped through feet first, and dropped to the cellar floor. She pushed the window shut, then jammed her knife into the lock.

She held her breath, sinking against the cold basement wall. But no dead pounded on the window. She listened for movement above. A creak of floorboards was followed by a haze of dust filtering through the air. Voices drifted downward into the basement, but she could not make out the words.

She blinked a few times to clear a welling of tears and allow her eyes to adjust to the dim light. Around her, shelves lined the basement. Ellie grabbed her pack and stuffed it behind a shelf, adjusted her rifle, then crept toward the staircase. Close to the first step, attached to the foundation wall, was a large circuit panel. Beneath it lay a row of large battery packs atop a wooden platform—storage cells for solar panels, likely on the roof.

Ellie raised the rifle barrel and pressed a foot on the first step. It creaked. After a brief pause, she continued up with a slow, careful placement of her feet on the treads. The door at the top was closed, but the doorknob turned freely. She gave it a gentle nudge. The door opened an inch or two. She squinted through the crack. Down the dimly lit hallway, a number of people spoke in a bantering tone that was scattered liberally with expletives, their shadows snaking across Ellie's narrow scope of vision. None of the voices were from the couple that had been part of the community for so many years. She slid back into the darkness, pressing against the wall.

Her right pointer finger tapped against the rifle just above the trigger.

Stay on mission, Charlie drilled into her many times over. *Fubar happens when you get distracted, and you can't afford a mistake.*

She rubbed at her nose with the back of her hand. A spitting sound caught Ellie's attention. She leaned closer to the door. A radio speaker spat again when someone released a microphone.

"They'll be coming right down the road," a woman said. "Right into town."

"No, they won't," retorted a man's voice. "We've got a thaw going. And a herd. Goddamn, it's early in the year. They won't get through."

"Shut your piehole," another man said. "They want to rescue those people, they'll get through. And we own both sides of the road."

They moved around, accompanied by mumbles and grumbles.

"And just how do we get across to those houses?" the first man asked. "There's too much traffic out there."

"Back door," another woman said. "Circle farther up the street."

Feet creaked the floorboards again.

"Good angles on the street," said a different man's voice, a deep gravelly sound. "Get them in the cross-fire. Fish in a barrel."

The room broke out into noisy discussion, making the voices harder to follow. Through the growl and the high-pitched questions, the radio crackled, followed by a familiar EMT's voice. "We'll be ready for the ride. Yes, you have our location."

A hush fell across the room.

A nameless voice followed a click of static. "You're sure the herd cleared?"

"A few remain, but nowhere near the numbers. By the time you get a few vehicles there, they will have mostly moved along."

"Very good," said that nameless voice. "We'll assess the situation once we get there, juncture of Routes 322 and 528."

"Roger that," Mark acknowledged.

The radio fell silent.

"They could be about fifteen to twenty minutes if the snow has melted sufficiently," the first male voice said. "If they have to dig their way through, could take a few hours."

"There's sufficient snow on the road to the west," said the first female voice. "With the rain, it'll be heavier. They'll need equipment to clear a path."

The floorboards creaked with footfalls, the voices again melding into a confusion of words. Someone approached the cracked door. But the steps passed without so much as a pause.

Ellie crouched at the bottom of the staircase, pulling magazines from her backpack and stuffing them into her pockets. She stowed her flashlight back into her pocket. A distant back door opened and swung shut. Whatever number of them that spilled from the old general store, they would likely move quickly to keep the herd from returning.

Remember, the enemy always gets a vote, Charlie said again.

She rested the rifle across her knees and closed her eyes. Her already shattered world had fallen into complete pieces when she found her brother stretched across a monument to the heroes of a world that no longer existed. She clenched the cold steel in her hands, its black surface familiar beneath her fingers—but she had never taken a human life with it.

She stared at the cast-iron sights on the barrel, her skin growing cold.

Dear God, she thought, *why did you have to go for supplies, Charlie? We had enough to spare.* But in the end, she could not blame her brother for whatever had occurred. It comforted her to imagine that he had died for something, or someone.

She painfully rose to her feet and crawled up the stairs to the landing. Through the cracked doorway, she could see a figure standing before the window overlooking the main street. She drew the kitchen knife and opened the door just enough to slip into the hallway's shadow. She took one step, then another. Pain stole her breath.

She ground her teeth together, fighting the urge to exit through the back door and shelter in the school until she could return to the farm. There was nothing keeping her here, for this was not her fight. She had cleared the road. They could not ask more of her. And then she saw the glow of the light from the radio. The EMT likely still sat at the other end with Sammy standing nearby.

Fubar, she repeated in her head, imagining Charlie's watchful eyes upon her. An unseen hand had already cast the die.

Ellie crept closer to the main room where the shelves and counter became visible. Against the front window stood a slender figure dressed in an oversized winter coat. A thicket of hair tumbled down her back. This woman peered through a pulled-back curtain at the houses across the street.

In the distance, an audible rumble grew closer.

Ellie adjusted her sweaty grip on the knife hilt and stepped forward again. Then she froze. The woman raised her hand to rub at her nose. Just when her hand fell to her side, the woman turned. Her eyes met Ellie's. In the space of a heartbeat, the woman fumbled for a pistol, but when she raised it, Ellie was gone.

"Someone's here!" she yelled.

The footfalls pounded in the hallway above.

Ellie crawled behind the clerk's counter while the woman swept through aisles of shelves that crowded the room. A crack sounded, deafeningly loud. Splinters flew near Ellie's head. She threw herself across the aisle and pressed against the endcap. The woman fired wildly in her direction. Ellie held her breath, expecting a round to tear through her body in a jarring fade to black. When the woman stepped around the edge of the aisle, Ellie stabbed her boot, driving the blade through leather and into the thick rubber sole.

The pistol clattered to the floor. Ellie snatched it, driving it up under the woman's chin when she crumpled over. The woman awkwardly swiped at it. The gun barked with an explosion of brains and blood.

"Oh... God," Ellie blurted, dropping the weapon, the barrel still smoking.

Feet pounded down the stairs.

A tall slender man appeared, in his shaking hands a hunting rifle, his face lean and unshaven. Dark circles haunted his eyes.

"I know you're here," he said, raising the rifle and scanning the aisles.

But that surveying stopped when his eyes met Ellie's through the GI sights of the long, black rifle. However, that barrel didn't waiver, her finger on the trigger. He raised one of his hands, then dropped the hunting rifle

Ellie waved her barrel to direct him away from the weapon.

His head bobbed and he tipped the rifle with his boot, then he shuffled aside. Ellie kept her sights pointed to his center mass. Carefully creaking across the floorboards, she swept a shelf near the service counter and hooked a finger around a roll of duct tape. With a slight motion of the barrel and gesture with her head, she directed him toward an armed chair near the hallway.

"He will kill you. You know that?" the man grumbled with a scratchy voice.

Ellie shrugged.

"And I'll shoot you where you stand," she replied.

His face drooped. He dropped into the chair. She tossed him the tape.

"Get it done," she ordered.

He bent and, with a sticky rip across his ankles, the tape wrapped around the chair legs. Then he tugged it around his wrist a few times, leaving the roll hanging.

"Up to you now," he said with a frown.

"Hand on the other arm," she demanded.

He complied.

Ellie pressed the rifle to the side of his head, her finger on the trigger, then wrenched the roll to tear it loose. It wrinkled, but she dragged the tape across his body to his other arm and quickly finished off the task. She cut the roll free with her knife.

"Did you kill my brother?" she asked, her voice low. But the confusion on his face caused her to continue. "You slaughtered everyone, but you strung up my brother."

"The guy in the park? Killed three of us before we knew he was here. Me and Sarah didn't want anyone hurt."

"Who did that?" she insisted.

But a gunshot cracked outside the store, followed by another.

She taped over his mouth.

Crouching beneath the windows for cover, Ellie returned to the woman's corpse, snatching up the pistol. She stuffed it into her jacket pocket, then scrambled when a round blew through the front window, glass crackling on the floor.

A diesel engine rumbled closer, and Ellie peeked from the corner of the window. Outside, a snowplow broke through a drift of wet snow and the truck came under fire from across the street. The cutting edge of the plow came to rest amid a pile of churned over body parts. Inside the cab, both driver and passenger ducked beneath the doors. An ambulance careened to a stop behind the truck.

Ellie crawled around the aisles to the staircase. A round again scattered glass and threw splinters across the counter.

The man taped to the chair burbled through the swath covering his mouth. ". . . string you up . . . your brother!"

But Ellie continued up the stairs then across a hallway and into the front bedroom. Gunfire quieted. The ambushers would need to storm those very vehicles to overcome the personnel hunkered inside them.

The window had been opened by the previous occupant in anticipation of the ambush. Ellie grabbed a pillow from the bed, rumpled it up beneath her throbbing knee, then pressed her body against the wall to minimize her silhouette. Her hands trembled when she lifted the rifle, barrel swinging out just over the windowsill, her heart pounding wildly in her head. Once she pulled the trigger, there would be no turning back—she would become the target. She had never before aimed a weapon at a living human with intent to kill. And now she stared down the long black barrel of the .308 to do harm. Bile rose in her throat, and the churning in her stomach threatened to erupt.

Focus, Charlie's voice hissed in her ear. *Let your breath out slowly.*

A man slipped out the side door of the house directly across from her, a rifle against this shoulder, sweeping the length of the two vehicles with its barrel.

Center mass, Charlie's voice continued. *Don't focus on anything else, then squeeze the trigger. Don't jerk on it, just squeeze.*

When she finished exhaling, the rifle barked and bucked. The sharp smell of gunpowder bit her nose in a grey wisp of smoke, the shell casing clattering to the floor. Across the street, the man jerked and fell to the ground. Ellie withdrew inside the window.

Shouts broke out.

She crawled across the room to another window, then pulled the curtain back to peek out once more. When the personnel moved in the vehicles below, gunfire resumed. From a window above the porch on the second floor, a woman stirred the curtain, then fired down on the lead vehicle. The window opened with a screech. Ellie rested her elbows on the sill, lining up the cast-iron post into the target window.

Do not look at her face, she told herself. *Center mass—eyes focused. Do not look at her face.*

A deep breath filled her lungs, then she slowly exhaled. She began to squeeze the trigger. Splinters shattered near her head.

Ellie plunged to the floor, her knee screaming beneath her.

Keep moving. Charlie's voice was clear through the chaos in her head.

Another bullet ripped through the glass, showering her with shards.

She dragged herself to the other window, then held her breath for a few moments before peeking out the edge. The woman fired down on the vehicles. Ellie raised the rifle then framed the woman in the sights once more, placing the post in the center of her chest. The air was warm when she sucked it in and released it, squeezing the trigger once more. Rounds erupted around Ellie. This time the woman did look up and her way. Ellie saw her face in the sights, and the .308 bucked, ejecting another round with a clatter.

Ellie dropped to the floor.

She choked for air.

The woman's eyes had met Ellie's before her face slackened, blood erupting behind her. A puff of smoke from the round stung Ellie's eyes.

A door on the first floor beneath Ellie burst open, rattling the floorboards.

The prisoner chattered unintelligibly. A crack echoed through the house.

On the stairs, footfalls fell heavily. Ellie dragged herself upright, fumbling to bring the rifle to the ready. The man who exploded into the room was tall and thick, his ruddy, square face flushed. In his hands was a rifle, the mirror of Ellie's own, its surface black and the barrel quickly snapping up with angry eyes staring down the barrel into Ellie's face.

"Who the hell are you?" he demanded, spittle flying through the air. While he was a large man, he looked very ordinary in plain blue jeans and a winter jacket that could have been found at a local feedstore or stripped from the body of a farmer. But his boots—those black jump boots were familiar—and, for a split second, she believed she would find Charlie's name on the bottom, written with a white permanent marker.

"His ... his sister," she stammered.

He stopped in the doorframe.

"What? That makes no sense." His teeth ground together.

Ellie raised her hands from her own rifle.

"Your friend said you killed my brother. Strung him up without putting him down."

A grin cracked the crags in his cheeks, and he spit on the floor.

"That son of a bitch? Pulled his guts out of his body and tied them into a knot. He screamed like a baby for hours before he turned. So, you've come to even the score, eh? Goddamn, girl, I'm going to enjoy this first."

A shot burst out of Ellie's jacket, striking the doorframe. She pulled the trigger again and again, the hot metal casings burning her hand. The man jumped to the side while Ellie moved without knowing if she hit him. He was quickly upon her. His balled fist struck her on the side of the face, throwing her against the window, the remaining shards of glass and the wood frame cracking with the impact. She grabbed the molding with one hand and slammed the butt end of the .308 into his jaw. He roared, spitting blood.

"You killed my brother!"

Ellie swung the rifle barrel up on the pivot of her rifle sling. Without room to sight or maneuver, she pulled the trigger again, and again, and again.

The dump truck barreled through the snow, the heavy plow scraping ice and pavement with a cascade of slush. An ambulance followed in the truck's wake. The hospital crew tumbled from the vehicles with crowbars and baseball bats in hand, making short work of the dead that congregated around the chugging generator. The stolid EMT, Mark, ran down the stairs to greet them. Sammy appeared from the attic at the top of the garage steps, then slowly raised a hand.

Ellie remained in the plow truck's center seat, unmoving while the first of the patients were assisted from the home. Her eyes stared numbly across the hood of the vehicle, listening to the circulator fan rattle in the dash. Suddenly an urge to escape recycled air came upon her, and Ellie tumbled out of the truck, rifle swinging from her neck.

She wiped at her nose with the back of her hand.

The hills of Ohio were no strangers to the fickle weather, particularly in the late winter. But a cold front was on the wind, and the morrow would be frigid when it passed through. Already the air carried with it the promise of fresh early spring snow.

Ellie blinked but refused to close her eyes longer than necessary for Charlie's tormented face appeared—or the face of the woman in the store at the moment her head painted the room. She rubbed her eyes, for the flash of images always ended with the woman's eyes through the GI sights. Ellie stood at the tailgate, lifting her hand to open the rusted latch. But her fingers refused to close on the cold metal. She dragged that same hand up to her cheek and tiredly tugged a loose strand of hair behind her ear.

The latch to the dumper clanged free when she finally tugged on it. Ellie covered her eyes with her free hand, not wanting to look where Charlie lay in a black body bag. She was alone, for until then she had carried on with the hope he would return.

She whirled around at the sound of a footfall in the slush.

Sammy raised his hands, hobbling to remain upright.

"It's just me—it's just me..." he said. He looked over her shoulder at the truck's cargo. "Charlie? I'm so sorry, Ellie."

He closed his mouth, even though she knew he had more to say. Charlie had been an older brother to so many of her friends. The pain on his face was palpable, forcing Ellie to look away.

"I need to get him home," she said.

Sammy's head bobbed in agreement.

Ellie dragged herself up into the truck dumper bed. She approached the body bag with a bit of trepidation. A shuffling sound at the gate caught her attention. She glanced over her shoulder, and there the hospital crew crowded around Sammy. Mark grabbed the side of the truck bed, pulling himself up.

"You don't have to go back," he said, but the response on her face encouraged him to change tack. "If you do, you don't have to go back alone."

He gestured a bit desperately to the plow driver, a tall, lean woman. "Let them look at that knee. Then we can navigate that road to get you home."

"I can't ask…" Ellie began.

"You didn't have to ask," the EMT said.

Blood rushed to Ellie's cheeks.

Hands reached up to assist her as she lowered herself to the ground.

The hospital personnel efficiently loaded the patients, while another EMT shepherded Ellie to an ambulance and examined her knee. The woman's cold fingers probed the swelling.

"Nothing but a sprain," she pronounced, spreading some ointment on the swollen joint, then wrapping it in a bandage. "Take things carefully for a couple of weeks. Come with us."

"I can't," Ellie replied with a bit of regret. "I have so much to do."

"You need time to heal."

"She won't be alone," Sammy said. "I'm going with her."

"You can't!" Ellie blurted. "Chemo . . ."

Her friend grinned. "I told you, finished my last treatments."

"No!" Ellie pulled away from the EMT, tugging her pant leg back down over her knee.

Sammy watched her limp a step or two.

"Can't what?" he asked.

"I can't put you down," she whispered.

"What? What do you mean?"

"You need to go with them. You deserve a good life."

Sammy touched her shoulder. "I've got no one. There is no good life."

"That's why you can't come with me!" she barked. "I can't... I can't put you down. Not like Charlie."

He rubbed his scruffy chin for a moment.

"I can't promise you won't have to someday," he replied. "But I'd rather spend what time I've got left with you."

She wiped at her eyes with the back of her hand.

"You're my memory . . . you know, of life before," she admitted. "I've got so few left."

"I'm still me. Please, I don't want to live . . . or die alone."

A strand of her hair tickled her forehead. She blew it aside.

"I do still believe," she admitted to Sammy.

And for the first time in a very long time, she felt closer to that world which no longer existed—and she knew it never would again.

TOUCH OF THE POET'S PEN

Do I bleed the drops of blood
that unbidden fall,
uncut rubies of emotion and pain?
Do they drip from my body,
red rain—
my thoughts and fears
to the yellowed surface scribed?
Do they stain, do they stain,
and blacken with time?

The wounds heal and mend—
yet remains the darkened page.

AUTHOR'S NOTES

This volume resulted from the encouragement from my daughter, Gwen, who after the release of *The Silver Horn Echoes: A Song of Roland,* wanted me to release the stories that she remembered from childhood.

Many of these tales have not seen the light of day since I was much younger studying in college or focused on raising our children. However, *What's in a Name* and *The Lost Spell* were more recently published as stand-alone tales. While proofreading, and rewriting, Gwen encouraged me to also craft another story for this specific volume. *GI Sights* grew from a concept that I had toyed with while engaged in author events in 2018 and 2019, particularly speaking with friends and colleagues while supporting the release of *The Silver Horn Echoes: A Song of Roland.* I wrote the piece during the first months of the COVID 19 pandemic, set in the familiar landscape of my youth in Huntsburg, Ohio.

You see, I grew up on a small farm in Ohio, and the summertime was oft a period of isolation, for we lived miles from the nearest town where many of my friends lived. Long days were filled with outdoor chores, exploring the surrounding woods, playing knights while on horseback, and camping in the woods behind our fields. Late into the night, I would lay in the tent reading. One of my favorites was a collection of short stories that included *Pigeons from Hell*, by Robert E. Howard. The smoldering campfire often cast long, twisted, dancing shadows while my imagination flew to distant lands.

While in college at BYU, I was very fortunate to participate in a creative writing class taught by Professor "Doc" Smith. Our short-story work led to a few of the pieces included here, but also to the origin chapter of the novel *Annwyn's Blood*. Those days of class, and my work on the *Leading Edge* magazine, were some of my cherished collegiate experiences.

Over the past few years, I've spent many hours on the road attending book festivals, comic cons, and author events, often listening and learning from other creators—authors and artists. While working on this collection, the addition of original artwork became a focus of this effort. Gwen stepped in to seek out the wonderful emerging artists who contributed to these pages. I am humbled by their creativity.

Finally, I want to thank all those who have encouraged me through the years. My wife, Lori, as well as my children who have never given up on my efforts. I love them for their understanding that this creative side is essential to who I am.

Writing provides me with sanity in the midst of the storms that blow across the seas of life.

So, here's to summertime campfires and the stories told in the deep of the night. May they continue to bring you to worlds yet to be discovered.

Michael Eging